KURT COBAIN AND MOZART ARE BOTH DEAD

KURT COBAIN AND MOZART ARE BOTH DEAD

THE SECOND *Leonard & Larry* COLLECTION BY

Tim Barela

Palliard
Press

Palliard Press   Minneapolis

2 3 4 5 6 7 8 9

Published by Palliard Press
c/o DreamHaven Books
912 West Lake Street
Minneapolis, Minnesota
55408

Book Design by Robert T. Garcia
with a special thanks to JDA Typesetting.

ISBN 1-884568-04-1

PRINTED IN THE UNITED STATES OF AMERICA
BOUND IN CANADA

For Bryan and Doug,
John and Skip

Good Friends and
Cherished Acquaintances,
Continuing Inspiration;
I will always
be glad that I knew you.

DISCOVERING THE WORLD OF LEONARD AND LARRY

BY ROBERT TRIPTOW

"How does it feel to be the one to have discovered Tim Barela?"

"Discovered? Who am I—Columbus? All I did was correct the spelling."

The question surprised me, but maybe the comparison between America and the world of "Leonard & Larry" is apt. Each was a whole world just waiting to be found and presented to society: big, real, funny, and fantastic. Anyone would have spread the word. All I had to do was put the best strip offered into a comic book I was editing.

I am proud that Tim was able to develop "Leonard & Larry" while I was editing *Gay Comix* in the 1980's. There he had the luxury of constructing well-rounded, longer stories where he could engage in lengthy banter and irony and shtick. Those are still my favorite "Leonard & Larry" stories (and are included in the previous collection, *Domesticity Isn't Pretty*)—and the copy editing is impeccable. *Gay Comix* later went into limbo, but Tim beautifully adapted the strip into a series of one-page installments for the gay press.

Not all subsequent publishers of "Leonard & Larry" fully appreciated its wonders, I'm afraid. The national newsmagazine *The Advocate* rather foolishly dropped it after a two-year run (the proofreading must have worn them out). Happily, the strip continues in *Frontiers* magazine. For now, anyway. You can never tell when some new, relatively comics-ignorant editor will come along and say, "That tired old thing? I don't even know which one is Leonard and which one is Larry!"

"Larry's the one with a beard."

"They *all* have beards! And Barela can't spell! Drop it!"

Confusing the continuity is a very real danger in a long-running narrative strip that appears only biweekly and features a growing number of characters and running jokes. A less-than-avid follower may read an installment about Larry's son's girlfriend's pregnancy—then not see an episode again until an unfamiliar cast includes concert pianists and closeted television actors. The scene may move from West Hollywood to Texas, of all places. Sheesh! Even Dickens, who originally published his novels as serials, had to remind his readers who was who. (He also had to proofread the spelling.)

You lucky people get to experience "Leonard & Larry" in the best possible way, as an uninterrupted continuity. You'll see the characters grow and change as their extended family keeps expanding. Everyone *ages,* a rare illustrative feat that has been carried off successfully only in the newspaper strips *Gasoline Alley* and *For Better or For Worse.* That puts Tim Barela up there with the masters of cartooning (even if he can't spell). Although I'm sure that Leonard and Larry themselves *might* prefer to live in one of those cartoon worlds where no one gets any older.

"So which character is Tim Barela—Leonard or Larry?"

That's a good question, and the answer is: "Neither. Both." All of his characters are little pieces of Tim. God knows he can be as fussy as Leonard, and he dresses like Larry. The first time I met him, it was like seeing Francis Ford Coppola in black leather (the big difference is that Coppola gets more money for his storytelling). Of course Tim had a beard. And he struck me immediately as an unusual fellow.

He's unique among cartoonists in that he wasn't heavily influenced by comic books as a child. Tim is a television kid (which may explain his inability to spell). In essence, "Leonard & Larry is a sitcom. Leonard and Larry are the offspring of Lucy and Ethel, our Miss Brooks, Darren and Samantha, Rob and Laura, Mary and Rhoda, Archie and Edith, and Sam and Diane. They and their friends are descended from *Abie's Irish Rose, Father Knows Best,* and Donna Reed. They're originally from Mayberry, they've hung out at Cheers, are on a nodding acquaintance with Murphy Brown, can out-bitch the cast of *Designing Women,* and have French-kissed Roseanne.

My one complaint about "Leonard & Larry" is that virtually all of the mail that came to *Gay Comix* during that period and bothered to mention *my* cartooning said, "I like your stuff. Please forward my fan letter to Tim Barela." Correspondence to a guy who once actually misspelled his own name! *I'm* the one who corrected his typos—you'd think Tim could at least include my visage as a "Leonard & Larry" cameo character, as he's done with other friends.

It will never, happen, though.

I don't wear a beard.

THE CAST OF CHARACTERS—SO FAR

It's a big cast and getting bigger. For those of you who haven't recently read "Leonard & Larry" and don't have the time to flip through *Domesticity Isn't Pretty*, the previous volume, here's a recap of the characters who appear again in the book you're now reading. You're going to meet a bunch of new people, as well, but I'll let you discover them for yourselves in Tim's excellent pages.

►**Leonard Goldman**, b. 1953, is a fashion photographer and something of what we in the ghetto call a "guppie," a gay yuppie. He's actually worn polo shirts and cloth belts. He and Larry live in West Hollywood.

◄**Larry Evans**, b. 1952, runs a leather shop on Melrose Avenue and wears his wares. Late to emerge from the closet, he was married for eight years and fathered two sons. He eats too much chocolate and has a screwball temperament.

LARRY'S RELATIVES

►**Richard Evans**, b. 1975, Larry's older son, (his mother calls him by his middle name, Michael). You can tell Richard isn't gay because he's one of the few men in the strip who doesn't have a beard. Richard and his girlfriend had a baby and married immediately after their high school graduation.

SAY, DAD, WOULD YOU LIKE SOME COFFEE? YOU LOOK LIKE YOU COULD USE SOME...YA KNOW, YOU REALLY TIED-ONE-ON AT YOUR BIRTHDAY PARTY LAST NIGHT. I DON'T THINK I'VE EVER SEEN YOU DRINK LIKE THAT BEFORE.

UGGHH...DAVID?...DAVID! MY SON, FRUIT OF MY LOINS, YOUNGEST OF MY CHILDREN. LOOK AT YOU! YOU HAVE A MUSTACHE AND YOU'RE AS TALL AS I AM...MY GOD, EITHER YOU'VE GROWN OR I'M SHRINKING! THAT'S WHAT HAPPENS TO OLD FOLKS, YOU KNOW. I'M FORTY, NOW; I CAN PRACTICALLY FEEL THE TIRED OLD CELLS, IN THESE TIRED OLD BONES, COMPACTING.

◄**David Evans**, Larry's younger son, b. 1977. A couple of years ago, David shocked his father by revealing that he too, was gay. And publicly gay at that, as he and his boyfriend Collin made headlines by suing the Anaheim school board so they could attend their junior and senior proms together. For that, they were "bashed" while walking along the beach, holding hands

➤**Sharon Delbart Evans**, Larry's ex-wife, who has become more understanding about homosexuality with time and experience—despite living in Orange County. After all, her ex-husband, her son, and even a former fiancé all turned out to be gay (and bearded, too). Can this woman pick 'em or what?

SHARON, MY FAMILY HAS HAD A HARD ENOUGH TIME WITH THE IDEA OF ME MARRYING A DEVORCÉE...I SWEAR, MY MOTHER WOULD HAVE A COW IF SHE FOUND OUT THAT I WAS ABOUT TO BREAK BREAD WITH YOUR EX, AN ADMITTED HOMOSEXUAL, AND HIS...HIS LOVER; THE TWO OF THEM LIVING HERE ...IN SIN!

THIS IS WEST HOLLYWOOD.

SAME DIFFERENCE!

IF YOU LIKE, DEBBIE, I CAN SET A FORK OUT FOR YOU.

OH NO, IT'S COOL. I MEAN, LIKE, THESE DAYS, ONLY DOOFUSES AND DWEEBS DON'T KNOW HOW TO EAT WITH CHOPSTICKS. LIKE, I'M TOTALLY NORMAL.

◄**Debbie Dunbarton Evans**, Larry's daughter-in-law, is something of a sweet hothead, quick to anger, quick to the defense of what's right for her loved ones. She surfs too.

➤**Lauren Phylicia Evans**, Richard's and Debbie's daughter, b. 1991 (on Larry's birthday). She's two years old at the start of this batch of "Leonard & Larry" cartoons. They grow up so fast.

GOODNESS, GRACIOUS, LAUREN, BUT DON'T WE —OW!—HAVE BUSY LITTLE —AGGGH!— HANDS TODAY! MAYBE YOUR GRAN'PA LEONARD WOULD LIKE TO— OUCH!—HOLD YOU FOR AWHILE.

NO WAY.

LEONARD'S RELATIVES

➤**Esther Goldman**, Leonard's traditionally Jewish mother, always with the chicken soup—and matchmaking, until she finally realized that her baby had already met his match. She was present at the birth of *Larry's* granddaughter because it was the closest she would get to a grandchild from Leonard himself. "and I'm not missing it for the world!"

MOM, NORMAN AND BERNIE HAVE GIVEN YOU **FIVE** GRANDCHILDREN WHO, OVER THE YEARS, HAVE CONTINUALLY TAKEN ADVANTAGE OF YOU LIKE A **GANG** OF LITTLE **EXTORTIONISTS.** **WHY** WOULD YOU WANT **ANOTHER?**

SO THAT I COULD HAVE SOMEONE ELSE BESIDES **YOU** TO **BREAK MY HEART,** DEAR.

HERE IT COMES! REMEMBER, YOU CAME ALONG TO GIVE ME **MORAL SUPPORT.**

AND TO HELP YOUR BROTHER, BERNIE, **POLISH OFF** THE **KNISHES.** IN THE MEANTIME, YOU'RE ON **YOUR OWN.**

◀**Bernard Goldman**, Leonard's second-older brother, a television screenwriter. We really didn't get to know him in the previous strips, but he plays an important part in the success of Merle in this book. Who's Merle? Keep reading!

THE IN-LAWS

➤**Phil Dunbarton** is Debbie's conservative father, whose narrow-minded opinions usually incite his daughter's wrath (and set us up for Tim's punchlines).

➤**Barbra Dunbarton**, Debbie's more understanding mother. We assume she doesn't use the usual spelling of "Barbara" because she's such a Streisand fan. Or Tim Barela is a Streisand fan. Or she's the victim of one of Tim's infamous misspellings. Or maybe it's just her name.

AVERT YOUR EYES, DEAR, AND JUST KEEP TELLING YOURSELF, "HE'S **ONLY** A RELATION BY **ACCIDENT OF MARRIAGE;** HE'S **ONLY** A RELATION BY **ACCIDENT OF MARRIAGE;** HE'S **ONLY...**"

FRIENDS AND ACQUAINTANCES

▲ **Bob Mendez**, a concert pianist, is currently recording a 14-CD series of Mozart piano concertos and bitching about every single note. He and Frank live in Long Beach.

▲ **Frank Freeman**, Bob's lover, an aerospace engineer, successfully fought the loss of his security clearance because of his sexuality. He wasn't quite as lucky later with across-the-board layoffs at his company. Oh well, he has his newly discovered fetish for uniforms to keep him happy, even if it drives Bob crazy.

◄ **Gene Slatkin**, Bob's friend and musical associate, a violinist and concert master for Bob's recording sessions. Heterosexual, incidentally, but he's got a gay attitude and, as Tim points out, a little beard.

► **Jim Buchanan** works at Larry's Leather on Melrose and has had a sad time of love. He lives with his cat, Smokey Bear, in Santa Monica. His last serious romance was given last rites when he discovered he was dating a Catholic priest—an episode which prompted a series of dream visitations from the ghosts of Jim's (and the cartoonist's) favorite composers:

Peter Ilyich Tchaikovsky and **Johannes Brahms** are classical composers who regularly haunt "Leonard & Larry" (Wolfgang Amadeus Mozart once made a cameo appearance). Tchaikovsky and Brahms are the only characters who understand that they're in a comic strip. They appear from time to time to comment on the story line and serve as a sort of "Greek chorus." What a comedown—from composing to the chorus.

Merle Oberon, a new friend from Texas. Oh, this story gets complicated. Some time back, we had a surprise visit from Larry's brother, "Bubba" Evans (real name: Dale), a trucker now residing in the Lone Star state. With him was Lucy-May Cogburn, his 18-year-old bimbo girlfriend, who dumped him the minute she met a movie producer. Ah, Hollywood. As soon as "Lucille May" and her bosoms appeared in *Ninja Babes Three*, her brother Van showed up with a friend to kidnap Lucy-May back to the cultural safety of Texas. The friend, one Merle Oberon, realized that West Hollywood suited him better than the Old West. Lucy's producer realized that Merle was a lot hotter than Lucy-May, too. Ah, Hollywood.

Nurse Mike, based on Tim Barela's friend Lurch, was introduced at the birth of Lauren in 1991. Like we needed any more reasons to dread a visit to the hospital?

Lillian Lynch, aggressive retail and real estate vampire, the proprietor of Manic on Melrose, who wants to buy out Larry's Leather. She once called our heroes at 2 a.m. to make them an offer. And some folks claim that gay people "recruit." She's usually seen with her silent, stoic man-Friday, "live-in boy toy," former Mr. Universe runner-up from Cancun, **Armondo Velenzsuela.**

13

Sullivan and **Miller** have a winery in Temecula, "S.&M. Cellars." We don't actually see them in this volume, and they only made a brief appearance in the past, but I'm mentioning them because we find out now that their first names are **Ed** and **Mitch** (the humor of which we discover only when we read all of the strips closely in one sitting). The real Mitch Miller, incidentally, was one of the few celebrities in America in the '50s to have a beard.

There's also an extended cast of interesting characters who were introduced in the past, appear fleetingly or not at all in this book, and may show up again in the future. For instance, **Collin**, David's boyfriend, is referred to but doesn't really show up in this collection. My guess is that he's off working on his moustache.

We'll have to wait for the next book for another visit from **Wilma** and **Earl Evans**, Larry's parents, of 14 Piccadilly Circle, The London Bridge Mobile Home Park, Lake Havasu City, Arizona. **"Bubba" Dale Evans**, Larry's younger brother, is probably pinching a waitress' butt in a coffee shop somewhere between here and San Antonio.

Meanwhile, Leonard's eldest brother **Norman** runs the family furniture business on Pico Boulevard, is married to **Irene** and raising their children, **Nathan** and the image-conscious **Rebecca**. And how are **Uncle Mendel** and **Aunt Sophie**?

And the rest of the extended gay family: **Lisa** and **Linda**, the lesbians Leonard's mother tried to match them up with. **Bennet**, Frank's son and Richard's teenaged friend. **Dennis** (Leonard's ex) and his boyfriend **Leon**. **Gordon Talbert**, the Moral Majority type from Anaheim who was revealed as a closet case known to some as "Sweet Cakes." What happened to them?

I think they're all off growing beards.

KURT COBAIN AND MOZART ARE BOTH DEAD

LEONARD, WHAT DO YOU THINK? IS THIS **TOO MUCH LEATHER?** DO THE ARM BANDS PUSH THE WHOLE-THING **OVER THE TOP?** MAYBE WITH-OUT THE CHAPS...

LARRY, IF YOU'RE NOT GOING TO WEAR IT, **WHY** DID WE **DRAG** ALL THAT STUFF WITH US, **THREE THOUSAND MILES?!**

...NOT TO MENTION HAVING TO **EXPLAIN** THE **CHAIN HARNESS**—WHICH YOU'VE NOW DECIDED **NOT** TO WEAR—WHEN YOUR CARRY-ON BAG SET OFF THE **METAL DETECTOR** AT THE AIRPORT.

WELL, I DO WANT TO WEAR **MOST** OF IT. IT'S JUST THAT THE MARCH TODAY IS SURE TO BE **CRAWLING** WITH THE **NATIONAL MEDIA.**

COME AGAIN?

YOU KNOW, ALL THOSE INTERSTATE **VIDEO VULTURES** WHO LIKE TO SENSATIONALIZE AN EVENT LIKE THIS BY FOCUSING ON ALL THE **DRAG QUEENS** AND **LEATHER.** THE NEXT THING YOU KNOW, SOME **CLOSET CASE** IN **COW'S BREATH, NEBRASKA** IS WRITING **ANN LANDERS** TO SAY THAT HE'S **NEVER COMING OUT** BECAUSE OF ALL THE **FREAKS 'N' WEIRDOS!** GEEZ, WHAT IF IT'S **ME** THAT THE GUY SEES?

That's **MR.** *Faggot to you, Sweetheart!*

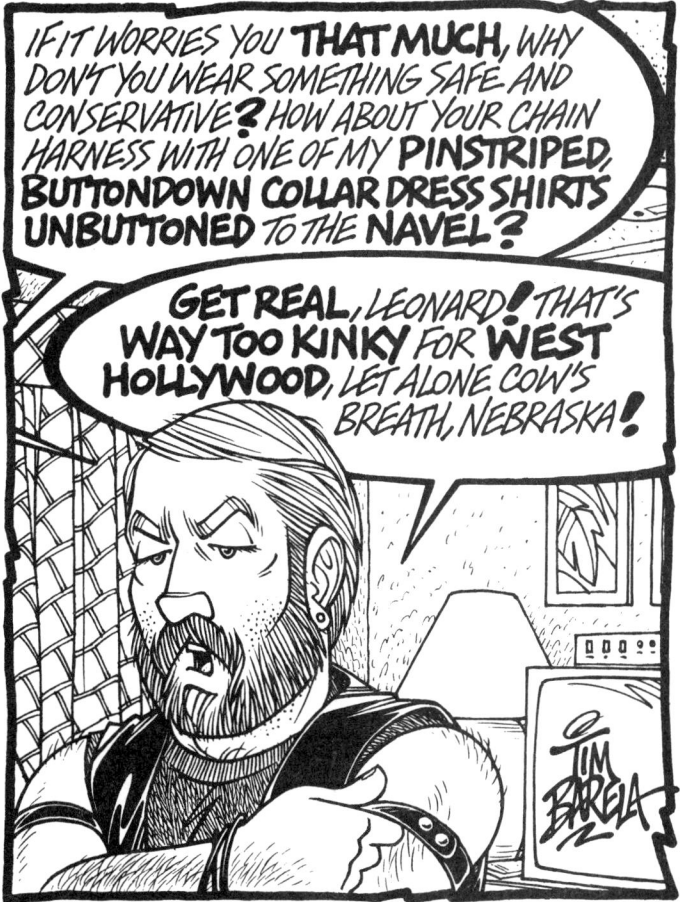

IF IT WORRIES YOU **THAT MUCH,** WHY DON'T YOU WEAR SOMETHING SAFE AND CONSERVATIVE? HOW ABOUT YOUR CHAIN HARNESS WITH ONE OF MY **PINSTRIPED, BUTTONDOWN COLLAR DRESS SHIRTS** UNBUTTONED TO THE NAVEL?

GET REAL, LEONARD! THAT'S WAY TOO KINKY FOR WEST HOLLYWOOD, LET ALONE COW'S BREATH, NEBRASKA!

17

Panel 1

PETER, WHY ARE WE HERE?

WELL, AFTER THE PATHOS AT THE END OF THE LAST BOOK, I SUPPOSE TO PROVIDE MINDLESS COMIC RELIEF.

NO, NO, NO! I MEAN, THIS PLACE. WE NORMALLY APPEAR IN THAT JIM FELLOW'S DREAMS. BUT THIS DOESN'T LOOK LIKE HIS APARTMENT IN SANTA MONICA.

HMMM... YOU'RE RIGHT. YET, THE VIEW OUT THE WINDOW SEEMS FAMILIAR. IT HAS CHANGED A BIT IN THE HUNDRED YEARS SINCE I WAS HERE LAST, BUT I COULD SWEAR THAT WE WERE IN NEW YORK CITY.

Panel 2

NEW YORK CITY?!

REALLY, JOHANNES, ALL YOU'D NEED IS A COWBOY HAT AND YOU'D BE A BAD SALSA COMMERCIAL! LET ME CHECK THE SCRIPT AND SEE WHERE WE MADE THAT WRONG TURN.

LEAVE IT TO A DIZZY QUEEN!

Panel 3

AH-HA! A PROTRACTED STORY LINE CONCERNING JIM IS ABOUT TO START, BUT WE WON'T BE NEEDED UNTIL THE VERY LAST EPISODE.

HMMM.... THIS WOULD SEEM TO BE GENE.... A VERY MINOR CHARACTER, MADE A BRIEF APPEARANCE IN EPISODE #64... A HETEROSEXUAL...

THEN WHO'S THIS?

Panel 4

A HETEROSEXUAL? I WAS UNDER THE IMPRESSION THAT THIS COMIC STRIP WAS FOR QUEERS ONLY! ...I SIMPLY MUST HAVE A WORD WITH THE MANAGEMENT!

YOU'RE STRAIGHT? REALLY? GREAT! I WAS BEGINNING TO THINK I WAS THE ONLY ONE AROUND HERE! THE NAME'S BRAHMS—J. BRAHMS—DEAD, GERMAN TUNESMITH. THAT ONE'S P.I. TCHAIKOVSKY, MUSICAL QUEER... CIGAR?

Panel 5

HMMM... APPARENTLY, GENE IS A CLASSICAL MUSICAN, A FRIEND OF THE CHARACTER WHO'S A CONCERT PIANIST—WELL, WELL!...IT SAYS THAT HE WAS MODELED AFTER THE ACTUAL CONCERT MASTER OF THE NEW YORK PHILHARMONIC WHO THE CARTOONIST SAW ON TELEVISION QUITE OFTEN AT THE TIME.

Panel 6

...CONCERT MASTER? THEN GENE, HERE, MUST BE A... A VIOLINIST!

EEEWW!!

Panel 7

TEMPERMENTAL LOT, THESE VIOLINISTS. FORCE THE POOR DEARS' FRAGILE EGOS TO STAND BY AND WAIT FOR A LITTLE OBOE SOLO AT THE BEGINNING OF YOUR ADAGIO AND THEY GO ALL MENTAL ON YOU!

THAT'S NOTHING. THE SOLOIST WHOM I DEDICATED MY VIOLIN CONCERTO TO DISMISSED IT ALL TOGETHER; HE PROCLAIMED IT, "UNPLAYABLE"!

WELL, THEY SAID THAT MY CONCERTO WAS, "MORE AGAINST THE VIOLIN THAN FOR IT".

Panel 8

SLAP!

WAY TA GO!

YEAH!

Panel 9

NEVER DID MUCH LIKE VIOLINISTS.

YEAH! SCREW 'EM IF THEY CAN'T TAKE A JOKE! LET'S GET OUTTA HERE.

WHAT THE HELL WAS THAT ALL ABOUT?!!

EEWWW! JUST WHAT IS THAT UGLY GREEN THING THAT LAUREN HAS?

GA'PA, GA'PA!

IT'S A BROCCOLI.

THAT SCRAWNY THING IS A BROCCOLI?

IT'S NOT FROM THE SUPERMARKET; I GREW IT. IN FACT, I WAS PLANNING ON HARVESTING SOME FOR DINNER.

WOOK, MOMMA, WOOK!

OH YUCK! THIS FILTHY THING IS FULL OF BUGS! I'M NOT GONNA LET YOU FEED BUGS TO MY CHILD!!

THOSE ARE APHIDS. THEY'RE THERE BECAUSE MY GARDEN IS ORGANIC —NO PESTICIDES. THE ONLY THINGS THAT GO INTO MAKING MY BROCCOLI ARE THE HONEST TOIL OF MY HANDS, THE GOLDEN CALIFORNIA SUNSHINE AND THE GOOD WEST HOLLYWOOD SOIL.

I SWEAR, EVER SINCE HE PLANTED THAT DAMN THING, HE'S BEEN SOUNDING MORE AND MORE LIKE MR. DOUGLAS ON "GREEN ACRES" EVERY DAY!

...ANYWAY, WE WERE SO PROUD OF DAVID AND COLLIN AT THEIR GRADUATION LAST MONTH... COLLIN WITH THAT PINK BANDAGE AROUND HIS HEAD AND ALL THE PEOPLE WHO CHEERED WHEN HIS NAME WAS CALLED.

YEAH... DAVID WILL BE ALL MOVED IN SOON. WITH COLLIN FINALLY OUT OF THE HOSPITAL, IT'S GOING TO BE REALLY NICE TO HAVE EVERYBODY OVER FOR A PARTY HERE AT THE HOUSE.

WELL, I THINK THAT IT'S A REALLY CUTE IDEA TO CELEBRATE LAUREN'S SECOND AND LARRY'S FORTY FIRST BIRTHDAYS TOGETHER. WE CAN HAVE A CLOWN CAKE AND HATS AND PARTY FAVORS AND PLAY GAMES LIKE "PIN THE TAIL ON THE DONKEY...

WHAT'S THIS? NOBODY TOLD ME ANYTHING...

HOW ABOUT "SPIN THE BOTTLE"? WE HAVEN'T HAD LARRY'S STORE MANAGER, JIM, OVER FOR A LONG TIME. THEN THERE'S THIS NEW FRIEND OF OURS WHO I WANT TO INVITE. HE JUST CAME TO L.A. FROM TEXAS LAST FALL; HE'S A REAL SWEETHEART. HIS NAME IS MERLE...

WHAT?! NO, NO, NO!!

...NO, LEONARD! I ABSOLUTELY FORBID YOU FROM PLAYING MATCHMAKER AGAIN! YOU KNOW GOOD AND WELL WHAT A BLOODY DISASTER IT WAS THE LAST TIME YOU TRIED TO PAIR-UP A COUPLE OF GUYS.

ARE YOU, BY CHANCE, REFERING TO ...US?

YOU KNOW WHO I MEAN, LEONARD... I SWEAR, THIS SORT OF THING IS A COMPULSION FOR YOU PEOPLE! SOME KIND OF JEWISH GENETIC THING WITH YOUR "Y" CHROMOSOMES.

MY "Y" CHROMOSOMES?

YES—"Y" AS IN YENTA!

...ANYWAY, AS I WAS SAYING, HIS NAME IS MERLE AND I THINK THAT JIM IS REALLY GOING TO LIKE HIM...

LEONARD, PLEASE! I DEPEND ON JIM. DO YOU REALIZE JUST WHAT KIND OF A BASKET CASE THAT MAN BECOMES WHEN SOME GUY DUMPS HIM?! ...OH, DISASTER!!

GOSH, DAD, I'VE ONLY BEEN MARRIED TWO YEARS. AFTER THIRTEEN WITH LEONARD, YOU SHOULD KNOW BY NOW THAT YOU CAN'T ARGUE WITH THEM.

...LEONARD JUST TOLD ME THAT THIS WAS A PARTY FOR **YOU.** SO IMAGINE MY **EMBARRASSMENT!** HERE I AM, DRESSED TO THE **KINKY NINES** IN LEATHER 'N' LATEX, AND I DISCOVER THAT IT'S ALSO A **KIDDY PARTY** FOR YOUR **TWO-YEAR-OLD GRAND-DAUGHTER!**

AW, DON'T SWEAT IT. LAUREN **LOVED** YOUR LATEX SHIRT. WE TOLD HER THAT YOU WERE "THE BALLOON MAN".

AND THEN, ON TOP OF EVERYTHING ELSE, IT'S **OBVIOUS** THAT THE ONLY REASON LEONARD INVITED ME HERE IN THE FIRST PLACE WAS TO TRY 'N' PLAY **MATCH-MAKER** WITH ME AND THAT GUY, MERLE.

...LIKE, I REALLY WANT TO GET INVOLVED WITH SOMEBODY ELSE RIGHT NOW. LIKE, I'M **STUPID ENOUGH** TO GO THRU ALL THAT **CRAP 'N' BULL SHIT** AGAIN—I'VE HAD IT; I'D **RATHER OPEN A VEIN!!** AND I DON'T CARE HOW CUTE HE IS!

...AND, I HAVE TO ADMIT, HE **SURE IS CUTE.** WHO'D HAVE THOUGHT THAT LEONARD COULD HAVE ME ALL FIGURED OUT **SO WELL?** I MEAN, MERLE JUST PUSHES **ALL** MY RIGHT BUTTONS! WHEN I FIRST SAW HIM STANDING THERE IN THAT **SEXY** GARTH BROOKS OUTFIT AND HEARD THAT **ADORABLE** ACCENT OF HIS, I SAID TO MYSELF, "GAAWD, THIS IS THE **MARLBORO** MAN OF MY DREAMS!"

...AND, HERE I AM, ALL DRESSED UP LIKE **GUMBY!!**

JIM! GET A GRIP, MAN, YOU'RE **LOSING IT! COURAGE** IN THE FACE OF ADVERSITY!!

...BUT WHO CARES?! WHO NEEDS A PHONY COCA COLA COWBOY LIKE THAT, ANYWAY? HE'D PROBABLY JUST WANNA **WALK ALL OVER** SOMEONE LIKE ME WITH THOSE **BIG, BEAUTIFUL BOOTS** OF HIS. HE'S PROBABLY EVEN **FORGOTTEN** MY NAME BY NOW.

HI... YER NAME'S **JIM** AIN'T IT?

UH...HI. THAT'S RIGHT, ...JIM. AND YOU'RE MERLE.

I KNEW IT WAS JIM! I THOUGHT I'D FERGET, BUT WHO COULD FERGET A GUY WEARIN' A **GREAT RUBBER T-SHIRT** LIKE THAT?

UH...DO YOU **LIKE** IT?

WELL, YEAH! IT'S **FUN.** IT KINDA LOOKS LIKE YER WEARIN' A BIG, BLACK **BODY CONDOM.** ...O' COURSE, I LIKE **THE PRESENT** A WHOLE LOT BETTER THAN I LIKE **THE WRAPPIN' PAPER.**

REALLY? UH...HOW ABOUT YOU 'N' ME GOING OUT FOR A **PIZZA?**

SURE, I LIKE **PIZZA.** BUT WE ALL'VE JUST BEEN STUFFIN' OUR FACES WITH BIRTHDAY CAKE 'N' DIM SUM 'N' POT STICKERS ALL EVENIN'!

WELL, THAT'S ONE OF THE NICE THINGS ABOUT **CHINEESE** FOOD; THERE'S **ALWAYS** ROOM FOR **PIZZA.** ...BY THE WAY, YOU'RE NOT A **PRIEST** OR ANYTHING, ARE YOU?

A PRIEST? ME? AW, **HELL NO!** I WAS BORN 'N' RAISED A METHODIST.

GOOD.

BINGO!

SHUT UP.

ALL THESE OLD BRICK BUILDIN'S SORT'VE REMIND ME OF GALVESTON.

THIS NEIGHBORHOOD IS CALLED OCEAN PARK. THERE USED TO BE THIS BIG OL' AMUSEMENT PARK DOWN ON THE BEACH WHERE THOSE TWO HIGHRISES ARE NOW. I CAN STILL REMEMBER RIDING THE ROLLER COASTER WHEN I WAS A KID...

VIVALDI'S PIZZA

HEY, TONY, MAY WE HAVE THE CHECK, PLEASE?

WHY, CERTAINLY SIR. AND MAY I JUST SAY THAT IT'S BEEN A PLEASURE SERVING TWO FINE GENTLEMEN SUCH AS YOURSELVES. COWBOYS AND KINKY QUEERS IN RUBBER ADD A CERTAIN AMBIANCE TO OUR LITTLE ESTABLISHMENT THAT I SIMPLY COULDN'T MANAGE ON MY OWN.

STOW THE SARCASM AND JUST GET THE DAMN CHECK!

JIM, YOU WERE SAYIN' SOMETHIN' A LIL' EARLIER ABOUT YOU LIVIN' SOMEWHERE 'ROUND HERE...IS IT VERY FAR?

UH...WELL, NOT THAT FAR. IT'S JUST FOUR BLOCKS UP THE HILL. YEAH, IT'S A GREAT LITTLE APARTMENT—RENT CONTROLLED...

...I'VE LIVED THERE FOR SEVEN YEARS, NOW, JUST ME 'N' SMOKY BEAR—MY CAT. YEAH, SEVEN YEARS IN THE SAME, GREAT LITTLE, RENT CONTROLLED APARTMENT HERE IN THE BEAUTIFUL PEOPLE'S REPUBLIC OF SANTA MONICA.

I'VE BEEN LIVIN' IN WEST HOLLYWOOD FER THE PAST FEW MONTHS WITH MUH FRIEND, LUCY, FROM TEXAS. SHE JUST GOT 'ER NEW PLACE 'N' AIN'T TOO KEEN ABOUT ME BRINGIN' TRICKS HOME. O' COURSE, LIVIN' ALONE, I DON'T S'POSE YOU'D HAVE ANY PROBLEM BRINGIN' HOME WHOEVER YA WANT... WOULD YA?

WHOA! RED LIGHT! HOLD IT RIGHT THERE! YOU KNOW WHERE ALL THIS IS GOING. SURE HE'S CUTE—HE'S GORGEOUS! BUT IS IT WORTH IT? ALL HE WANTS IS TO HAVE HIS WAY WITH YOU. HE'LL RIP OUT YOUR HEART 'N' STOMP THAT SUCKER FLAT! HE'S THE SAME AS ALL THE REST; DON'T GIVE IN!

UH...NO. NO PROBLEM AT ALL, MERLE.

GREAT! WHY DIDN'T YOU JUST OFFER TO MAKE HIM A KEY?! HAVE YOU LEARNED NOTHING FROM ALL THOSE LOUSY LIAISONS AND DISASTEROUS RELATIONSHIPS IN YOUR PAST?!

WELL, YA KNOW, I'VE HAD A REAL SWELL TIME TONIGHT. I THINK YER A SUPER NICE GUY, FUN TA BE WITH, GOOD LOOKIN'...HOW ABOUT, YA KNOW, ME 'N' YOU HEADIN' ON UP THAT HILL?...

WELL, UH...

BY THE WAY, YA DO HAVE PLENTY OF CONDOMS AT HOME, DON'T YA?

UH...NO, I DON'T THINK SO...BUT MAYBE TONY COULD TELL YOU WHERE YOU CAN FIND SOME.

ARE YOU OUT OF YOUR MIND?!! STOP ENCOURAGING HIM! STOP THIS NONSENSE RIGHT NOW, BEFORE IT'S TOO LATE!!

SAY, COULD YOU TELL ME WHERE I MIGHT BE ABLE TA BUY SOME CONDOMS?

WHY, CERTAINLY SIR. YOU'LL FIND THEM NEXT TO THE CASH REGISTER IN THE BOWL WITH THE AFTER DINNER MINTS. ...WHAT'S THIS PLACE LOOK LIKE, A FUCKING PHARMACY?!

UH...THERE'S A DRUGSTORE DOWN THE STREET.

I NO LONGER ASSUME RESPONSIBILITY FOR ANYTHING THAT MAY HAPPEN.

JIM BARELA

...BUT DON'T YA HAVE ANY REAL MUSIC? YA KNOW, STUFF LIKE TRAVIS TRITT OR DWIGHT YOAKAM OR BILLY RAY CYRUS...IS THIS ALL YA GOT? CHOPIN, TCHAIKOVSKY, MOZART, BRAHMS...HUH, AIN'T BRAHMS THE GUY WHO WROTE THAT OL' LULLABY?

BRAHMS WROTE MORE THAN TWENTY LULLABIES, AS WELL AS FOUR SYMPHONIES, TWO PIANO CONCERTOS, A VIOLIN CONCERTO, SONATAS, TRIOS, QUARTETS, QUINTETS, CHORAL WORKS, A MAGNIFICENT REQUIEM...

HUH...JUST LOOKS LIKE A FAT, HAIRY OL' MAN TA ME.

OK, LET'S NOT LISTEN TO MUSIC. WE COULD WATCH TELEVISION. SATURDAY NIGHT LIVE SHOULD BE ON ABOUT NOW.

BUT THERE'S NO T.V. IN HERE.

THAT'S BECAUSE IT'S IN THE BEDROO— UH, OF COURSE, THE NEW SATURDAY NIGHT LIVE JUST DOESN'T COMPARE WITH THE GOOD, OL' ORIGINAL SATURDAY NIGHT LIVE...ON SECOND THOUGHT, LET'S NOT.

...WATCH T.V., THAT IS. WE CAN JUST SIT HERE, INSTEAD, AND VISIT. YOU KNOW, GET TO, UH...KNOW EACH OTHER BETTER.

SOUNDS FINE TA ME. VISITIN' ON A COUCH IS ONE O' MY FAVORITE PASTIMES. O' COURSE, I HOPE THAT TRIP TA THE BEDROOM IS STILL ON THE ITINERARY FER LATER.

...AND NOT TA WATCH SATURDAY NIGHT LIVE, NIETHER. JIM, SOMEHOW, I DON'T THINK THAT YOU INVITED ME AWAY FROM LARRY'S BIRTHDAY PARTY SO WE COULD END UP HERE AT YER PLACE 'N' WATCH "THE CHURCH LADY". HELL, I COULDA STAYED HOME IN TEXAS 'N' VISITED WITH MY MOMA'S FRIENDS FER THAT!

UH...WHAT ARE YOU DOING?

JUST GETTIN' COMFORTABLE; TAKIN' MY BOOTS OFF. O' COURSE, I S'POSE A GUY LIKE YOU LIKES IT BEST WHEN A FELLA LIKE ME KEEPS HIS BOOTS ON...I LIKE IT, TOO.

UH, DITTO...YOU'RE RIGHT, SOMETIMES I DO. I GUESS THIS MEANS I GO FIRST. WHAT ELSE WOULD YOU LIKE TO KNOW ABOUT ME? SHOULD I TELL YOU ABOUT THE PRIEST I DATED LAST YEAR? HOW ABOUT ALL THE OTHER TRAUMATIZING RELATIONSHIPS THAT I'VE BEEN IN AND OUT OF IN THE PAST TEN YEARS? YA KNOW, ALL THE SHIT I'VE BEEN THRU COULD MAKE A GUY SWEAR OFF SEX...

I BET YER REAL FURRY UNDER THAT HOT BLACK RUBBER...OOO! IS YER LEFT TIT PIERCED? DO YA LIKE IT WHEN I DO THIS?

OH YES! YEEES!! ...I MEAN, NO...DON'T. PLEASE DON'T...STOP.

...I MEAN IT, MERLE, PLEASE STOP.

I'M SORRY, MERLE. I THINK IT'S TIME FOR YOU TO GO HOME.

Panel 1:
...I KNEW THAT THIS WOULD HAPPEN; I KNEW IT, I KNEW IT! I COULD HAVE TOLD YOU, BEING DUMPED IS YOUR LIFE'S DESTINY. YOU SHOULD JUST STOP TRYING ALTOGETHER. LIFE WOULD BE SO MUCH EASIER FOR YOU...AND FOR ME.

...WHAT I CAN'T BELIEVE IS THAT, THIS TIME, THE WHOLE, GRUELING PROCESS TOOK JUST ONE NIGHT — YOU'VE BROKEN YOUR OWN RECORD!

MERLE DIDN'T DUMP ME, I TOLD HIM TO LEAVE.

LARRY'S LEATHER

Panel 2:
YOU DID WHAT?! ARE YOU OUT OF YOUR MIND? FOR ONCE, A HOT, HUNKY, HORNY MAN PRACTICALLY THROWS HIMSELF AT YOU AND YOU DUMP HIM?!...HELLO? IS ANYBODY HOME?

AW DAD, LAY OFF! CAN'T YOU SEE THAT JIM'S HURTING?

NO DAVID, IT'S OK, YOUR FATHER'S RIGHT. MERLE WAS THE MARLBORO MAN OF MY DREAMS AND I SENT HIM RIDING OFF INTO THE SUNSET ...WITHOUT ME.

Panel 3:
WOULD YOU LIKE TO TALK ABOUT IT?

DAVID, YOU WON'T GET THE CHANCE TO CRACK YOUR FIRST PSYCHOLOGY TEXT BOOK UNTIL YOU'RE OFF AT COLLEGE NEXT YEAR. I DON'T THINK IT'S WISE TO GET YOUR FEET WET PRACTICING ON A FULL BLOWN, RAVING, IRRATIONAL LUNATIC!... WHATEVER YOU DO, JUST MAKE SURE THAT ALL THE PIECES OF JIM'S LIFE ARE PICKED UP BY THE TIME I UNLOCK THE DOOR IN TEN MINUTES; I HAVE A BUSINESS TO RUN!

Panel 4:
I MEAN IT, JIM. I DON'T THINK YOU'RE CRAZY. WHY DON'T YOU JUST TELL ME WHAT HAPPENED. ...IT MIGHT HELP.

THERE ISN'T MUCH TO TELL. MERLE STARTED GETTING AMOROUS AND I TOLD HIM TO GO HOME BEFORE ANYTHING REALLY HAPPENED. THAT'S ALL. END OF STORY...WELL, MAYBE NOT... MERLE'S A REALLY NICE GUY, I LIKE HIM A WHOLE LOT AND I TOLD HIM SO...

Panel 5:
...BUT I WANT MORE THAN TO JUST BE ANOTHER ONE-NIGHT-STAND, THE OBJECT OF SOME GUY'S LUST, A CONQUEST FOR SOMEONE WHO WAS A STRANGER A COUPLE OF HOURS BEFORE—I'VE BEEN THERE TOO MANY TIMES...IT WOULD BE NICE—AND NOVEL—TO GO OUT ON A REAL DATE, SOMETIME. YA KNOW, DINNER AND A MOVIE AND A GOOD NIGHT KISS—PERIOD...I JUST WANT A REAL RELATIONSHIP, I WANT SOMEONE TO LOVE. SOMEONE TO BE THERE WHEN I COME HOME, SOMEONE I CAN COOK DINNER FOR, WHO I CAN ARGUE WITH AND MAKE UP WITH, SOMEONE WHO'LL HOLD ME WHEN I NEED HIM.

JIM BARELA

Panel 6:
...IS THAT SO MUCH TO ASK? TO HAVE WHAT YOU AND COLLIN HAVE, WHAT YOUR DAD AND LEONARD HAVE? I JUST WANT SOMEBODY TO LOVE ME! SOMEBODY WHO'LL—YA KNOW—BRING ME FLOWERS...SOMEBODY WHO'LL GO FOR A WALK WITH ME ON THE BEACH AND HOLD HANDS...

UH,... I WOULDN'T PERSONALLY RECOMMEND THAT.

Chap'n

23

Panel 1:
OH LOOK, JOHANNES, DON'T THEY MAKE THE SWEETEST COUPLE! ISN'T JAMES' NEW BEAU SIMPLY ADORABLE!

HUMPH. ISN'T THIS THE ONE WHO SAID THAT I WAS JUST A "FAT, HAIRY OLD MAN"? WELL, WE DIDN'T KNOW THAT THOSE UNFLATTERING OLD PHOTOS WOULD END UP, SOME DAY, ON ALBUM COVERS AND IN C.D. BOXES. WE DIDN'T HAVE ART DIRECTORS BACK THEN. I'M NOT MADONNA!

Panel 2:
...THINKS I'M A "FAT, HAIRY OLD MAN", DOES HE...

WELL, DEAR, MAYBE IT'S BECAUSE YOU ARE. WE COULDN'T ALL KEEP OUR BOYISH FIGURES. AND, THE BOYISH FIGURES YOU COULDN'T KEEP, YOU BOUGHT FOR TWO KOPECKS A TRICK ON THE STREETS OF MOSCOW!

Panel 3:
SHHH! YOU'RE GOING TO WAKE UP MERLE.

OH, NONSENSE! THIS IS YOUR OLD FRIEND TCHAIKOVSKY, DEAR...OH YES, AND BRAHMS...YOU'RE DREAMING—REMEMBER? HE CAN'T HEAR EITHER OF US.

PETE, JO—HEY, LONG TIME, NO SEE! WOW, AREN'T WE ALL DRESSED-UP, TONIGHT! THE TWO OF YOU GOING SOMEPLACE SPECIAL?

Panel 4:
"SOMEPLACE SPECIAL"? WHY, YES! SIMPLY THE GREAT PERIODIC GATHERING OF THE PANTHEON: THE ZENITH OF MUSICAL GENIUS, A COLLECTION OF SOME OF THE GREATEST CREATIVE SOULS WHO EVER LIVED.

AH, BUT TONIGHT IS INDEED SPECIAL! THIS YEAR, YOU KNOW, MARKS THE HUNDREDTH ANNIVERSARY OF MY PASSING AND, THIS EVENING, AN ORIGINAL ENTERTAINMENT BY GEORGE GERSHWIN AND LENNY BERNSTEIN WILL BE PERFORMED IN MY HONOR. OH, I'M SO EXCITED!

YEAH. IT'S OUR REGULAR THURSDAY NIGHT POKER GAME.

Panel 5:
...BUT THEN, WE ALWAYS HAVE FUN AT OUR LITTLE GET TOGETHERS. FOR INSTANCE, BEETHOVEN ALWAYS GETS STUCK WITH BEING IN CHARGE OF REFRESHMENTS AND HE ALWAYS GETS THE ORDERS WRONG..."I SAID THAT I WANTED 'A LITE'! WHAT'S THE MATTER WITH YOU, ARE YOU DEAF?!"...OH, WOLFIE AMADEUS AND I ALWAYS GET A CHUCKLE OUT OF THAT ONE.

EVERY BLESSED WEEK!

Panel 6:
WELL, COME ALONG NOW, PETER. YOU'RE GOING TO BE LATE FOR YOUR OWN PARTY.

OH, HE'S RIGHT. I REALLY MUST BE GOING. BUT CONGRATULATIONS, DEAR; THIS ONE'S A REAL CATCH!....IF ONLY I HAD BEEN AS LUCKY WHEN I WAS STILL UP AND KICKING. PERHAPS I WOULDN'T HAVE CHECKED OUT QUITE SO SOON.

THANKS, PETE.

Panel 7:
...IT REALLY IS REAL, THIS TIME...ISN'T IT?

GOSH, PETE, I SURE HOPE SO!

Panel 8:
JIM...JIM, YER TALKIN' IN YER SLEEP. ...WHAT'S "YO"? AND WHO THE HELL IS "PETE"?

HMMPH?... OH, JUST THIS REALLY OLD GAY MUSICIAN I KNOW...NEVER MIND, GO BACK TO SLEEP.

...THAT IS THE OFFICIAL OPENING SALVO FOR A PROJECTED FOURTEEN C.D. SERIES. OF COURSE, BOB HATES THE IDEA OF HIS LABEL PUTTING THE FOCUS ON HIM. BUT, AFTER BOB DID THAT SPOT ON THE TODAY SHOW, HIS PRODUCER AND ALL THE OTHER EXECUTIVE POWERS THAT BE REALIZED THAT THEY HAVE A REAL RISING STAR ON THEIR HANDS AND HAD BEST TAKE ADVANTAGE OF THAT FACT.

MOZART by MENDEZ
Piano Concertos 21 & 15
ROBERT MENDEZ

ISN'T IT AMAZING WHAT MAKING A FOOL OF YOURSELF WITH OL' WILLARD SCOTT ON NATIONAL TELEVISION CAN DO FOR YOUR CAREER.

SHE'S BACK! ALL I HAD TO DO WAS STICK MY HEAD OUT OF THE WINGS TO CHECK THE HOUSE AND THERE SHE WAS, AS USUAL, FRONT ROW, CENTER, SMILING THAT CREEPY SMILE AT ME!

WHAT? WHO'S BACK? WHAT ARE YOU TALKING ABOUT?

GIVE ME A BREAK, GENE! I CAN'T BELIEVE THAT YOU HAVEN'T NOTICED HER. YOU KNOW, THAT MUNCHKIN WITH THE FRIZZY HAIR, GLASSES AND BREASTS WHO'S SAT OBEDIENTLY AT THE FOOT OF THE STAGE FOR EVERY RECITAL THAT WE'VE GIVEN THIS WEEK IN LA JOLLA, SANTA BARBARA AND PASADENA.

...AND THAT'S NOT EVEN COUNTING THE TWO CONCERTS I DID WITH THE PACIFIC SYMPHONY DOWN IN ORANGE COUNTY LAST MONTH.

BOB, MAYBE SHE'S A MUSIC CRITIC OR SOMETHING.

OH NO, LEONARD, NOT HER! THAT WOMAN HAS "STALKER" WRITTEN ALL OVER HER SWEET PUDGY FACE! I KNEW THAT THIS SORT OF THING WOULD HAPPEN WHEN THEY INSISTED ON STICKING MY FACE IN THAT C.D. BOX!

BOB, BOB, BOB; ALWAYS LEAPING TO CONCLUSIONS. THE WOMAN IS MOST LIKELY NOT A STALKER—A FEW SCOOPS SHORT A FULL LOAD, MAYBE—BUT A STALKER, NO. THE REASON SHE'S BEEN FOLLOWING US FROM TOWN TO TOWN, ATTENDING ALL YOUR CONCERTS, IS PROBABLY JUST BECAUSE SHE LIKES YOU, SHE'S A FAN.

...ADMITTEDLY, A RATHER OBSESSIVE FAN. BUT, HEY, THAT'S JUST A PART OF THE PRICE OF SUCCESS. YOU'RE BECOMING A FAMOUS CONCERT AND RECORDING ARTIST; YOU HAVE FANS NOW; GET USED TO IT.

"GET USED TO IT"? HOW DOES ANYONE GET USED TO THIS SORT OF THING? BESIDES, HOW WOULD YOU KNOW? WHERE ARE YOUR LEGIONS OF GROOPIES? HOW WOULD YOU LIKE IT IF, SAY, SOME BIG, HAIRY FACED, CRAZED LOOKING THING STARTED COMING TO ALL YOUR CONCERTS AND GAVE YOU THE EYE ALL EVENING, MADE DESIGNS ON YOUR CROTCH?!

WELL, BEING THE TOKEN "BREEDER", I REALLY WOULDN'T KNOW HOW FLATTERING SOMEONE LIKE YOU MIGHT FIND SUCH A THING. HOWEVER, AFTER HANGING OUT HERE IN THE GREEN ROOM WITH YOUR FRIENDS, IT'S NOT AS IF I DON'T KNOW WHAT IT MIGHT BE LIKE.

LARRY!

HEY, I'M NOT DEAD YET.

26

Panel 1:
...YEAH, MERLE'S JUST ABOUT ALL **MOVED-IN**, NOW. AND YA KNOW, IF THERE'S ANYONE WHO DESERVES THE CREDIT FOR ALL THIS, IT'S **LEONARD**. LEONARD WAS **SO** RIGHT ABOUT GETTING ME AND MERLE TOGETHER! I ALWAYS KNEW THAT, SOMEDAY, THE RIGHT GUY WOULD COME ALONG, BUT I **NEVER** DREAMED THAT I COULD **EVER BE THIS HAPPY**!... I'M EVEN GETTING TO LIKE COUNTRY WESTERN MUSIC...

Panel 2:
WELL, SPEAK OF THE—THERE'S MY **BIG COWBOY** RIGHT NOW!... HOWDY PARDNER!

HI, **HONEY BEAR**!... YOU FERGOT YER **LUNCH**, SWEETNESS. I PACKED ALL YER FAVORITES, TOO: FRIED CHICKEN, MASHED POTATOES 'N' GRAVY, FRIED OKRA...

AWW, THAT'S MY THOUGHTFUL LOVER! YA KNOW, YOU'RE GOING TO MAKE ME **FAT** WITH ALL THIS **GREASY TEXAS LOVE.**

Panel 3:
WELL, THAT'LL JUST MEAN **MORE** O' YOU FER ME TA CUDDLE.... BUT DON'T YOU WORRY, NONE, WE HAVE **WAYS** TA MAKE YOU **WORK IT OFF**...MMMMM...

Panel 4:
(no text)

Panel 5:
ALRIGHT, ALRIGHT, BREAK IT UP! WE'RE **TRYING** TO RUN A **BUSINESS** HERE!!

AW HELL!...WELL, SO LONG, **SUGAR DARLIN**. I'M GONNA BE LATE FER MY AUDITION, BUT WE'LL BE SEEIN' YOU T'NIGHT. OH, I MISS YOU ALREADY!

I'LL BE COUNTING THE SECONDS, MY SWEET-HEART—I LOVE YOU!

Panel 6:
I HOPE YOU REALIZE THAT THAT **SHAMELESS LITTLE DISPLAY** WAS ABSOLUTELY **DISGUSTING**!

—SIGH— YEAH. ISN'T IT WONDERFUL?!

27

WHERE MAMA, DADDY, GA'PA? WHERE MAMA, DADDY?

I TOLD YOU, SWEETHEART, YOUR MOMMY 'N' DADDY ARE AT A CONCERT. THEY'LL COME BACK FOR YOU WHEN IT'S OVER. IN THE MEANTIME, GA'PA'S GOING TO FINISH GIVING YOU YOUR BATH AND THEN HE'S GOING TO PUT YOUR JAMMIES ON YOU AND FIX UP THE FUTON IN HIS ROOM SO THAT YOU AND YOUR TEDDY AND YOUR BUNNY CAN SLEEP ALL SNUGGLY-WUGGLY. DOESN'T THAT SOUND NICE?

...AND THEN THERE'S LUNCH. JIM USED TO GO OUT FOR A BURGER OR PIZZA. BUT NOW, EVERY DAY, HE JUST SITS NEXT TO THE MICROWAVE IN THE OFFICE WITH THIS BIG STUPIFIED GRIN ON HIS FACE, HEATING UP ONE USED BUTTER TUB OF DEEP-FRIED TEXAS NATIONAL DELICACIES AFTER ANOTHER.

AWW, THAT'S SWEET!

YEAH, RIGHT. GO AHEAD, LEONARD, GO AHEAD AND GLOAT OVER YOUR LATEST MATCHMAKING SUCCESS — GLOAT, GLOAT, GLOAT!

YOU KNOW, LARRY, SOONER OR LATER YOU'RE GOING TO HAVE TO DEAL WITH ALL THIS HOSTILITY YOU'RE HARBORING AS THE RESULT OF JIM AND MERLE'S RELATIONSHIP.

I AM NOT HOSTILE!!

BUT — GEEZ — LEONARD, YOU DON'T HAVE TO WORK WITH THE MAN! AND YOU DON'T HAVE TO LISTEN TO JIM READING ALOUD ALL THE DRIPPY LOVE NOTES THAT MERLE PACKS WITH HIS LUNCH: "I LOVE YOU; I MISS YOU; EAT ALL OF YOUR FRIED OKRA SO YOU CAN GROW UP TO BE BIG AND STRONG — TONIGHT"! AND THAT'S NOT THE WORST OF IT! YOU SHOULD BE SO LUCKY AS TO BE IN EARSHOT OF ONE OF THEIR SYRUPY TELEPHONE CONVERSATIONS; CUTESY PET NAMES AND MORON-ICALLY INSIPID BABY TALK FOR DAYS!

OUCH, GA'PA! HURT!

OH, I'M SORRY, PUNKIN! DID GA'PA GET SOAP IN HIS SWEET, PWECIOUS, WIDDLE BABY DOLL'S PUR IDDY-BIDDY EYE? — BAD, GA'PA, BAD!

...WUD YOU WIKE DUCKIE TO KISS IT AND MAKE IT BETTUR?

...I WUV YOU, YOU WUV ME, WE'RE A HAPPY FAMAWEE...

GIGGLE! GIGGLE!

...I MEAN, I KNOW THAT JIM AND MERLE ARE, SUPPOSEDLY, "IN LOVE" AND ALL, BUT — FOR THE LIFE OF ME — I DON'T THINK I'LL EVER UNDERSTAND WHAT COULD MAKE TWO GROWN MEN CARRY ON LIKE THAT.

WHO KNOWS. MAYBE THEY'RE SICK.

JIM BARELA

28

ARGGH! ROBERT, GET THIS MONSTER OF YOURS OFF OF ME!!

DOWN, BRUNO, DOWN! BAD, BAD, BRUNO! THAT'S NOT A REAL POLICEMAN, THAT'S JUST FRANK!

BARK! BARK! BARK! BARK!

DO YOU MEAN TO SAY THAT YOU SPENT HALF A FORTUNE ON A TRAINED GUARD DOG THAT—OF ALL THINGS—DOESN'T LIKE POLICEMEN?! GOOD LORD, WHAT DID THEY TRAIN HIM TO GUARD? A CRACK HOUSE?!

...AND WHAT HAPPENS NEXT MONTH, WHEN I GET TO HOST MY UNIFORM CLUB MEETING?!

DON'T WORRY, HE'LL BE SETTLED IN BY THEN—DOWN, BOY!—IF NOT, WE'LL JUST PUT HIM IN THE GARAGE OR SOMETHING.

BARK! BARK!

AND, FOR ALL THIS, WE HAVE YOUR PARANOID DELUSIONS OF SQUAT, BIG BOSOMED STAR STALKERS LURKING IN THE BUSHES TO THANK!

FRANKLIN, I HAVE BEEN SEEING THAT WOMAN EVERY-WHERE! AND NOT JUST IN THE AUDIENCE AT MY RECITALS OR WAITING BY THE STAGE DOOR, EITHER. LAST WEEK SHE WAS PARKED ALL DAY IN FRONT OF THE RECORDING STUDIO AND, JUST YESTERDAY, I SAW HER GOING THRU THE INTERSECTION OF BROADWAY AND XEMINO—BRUNO!—IN THAT VERY SAME RATTY ANCIENT VOLVO WITH THE BAD MUFFLER.

JIM BARELA

BOB, DIDN'T YOU STOP TO CONSIDER THAT, JUST MAYBE, THE WOMAN MIGHT LIVE HERE IN LONG BEACH, TOO?

OH NO, SHE DIDN'T SEEM FAMILIAR WITH HER SURROUNDINGS LIKE A "LOCAL", LIKE WHEN I SEE HER UP IN L.A. SHE WAS LOOK-ING FOR SOMETHING....AN ADRESS, A SIDE STREET—MIRA MAR AVENUE, NO DOUBT; SHE KNOWS WHERE WE LIVE!... MARK MY WORDS, FRANK, WHEN THAT NUT CASE REALLY IS JUST OUTSIDE OUR DOOR, "LURKING IN THE BUSHES" YOU'LL THANK ME FOR HAVING A LOYAL, TRUSTWORTHY FRIEND LIKE BRUNO STANDING OBEDIENTLY AT YOUR SIDE!

GRRROWL

AUUGGGH!! AND I JUST POLISHED MY BOOTS!!

BAD, BRUNO, BAD! THAT'S WHAT THE NEWSPAPERS ARE FOR!

AW GEEZ, IS THAT **SUNLIGHT** COMING THRU THE WINDOW? IS IT **MORNING ALREADY**? **CHRISTMAS MORNING?** ...UGGGH!...

IT'S HARD TO BELIEVE THAT I WAS **EVER YOUNG** AND **NAIVE** ENOUGH TO ACTUALLY **LOOK FORWARD** TO THIS DAY. OF COURSE, I'M OLDER AND **WISER** NOW; **FEAR AND LOATHING** IS **ALL** THAT I FEEL!

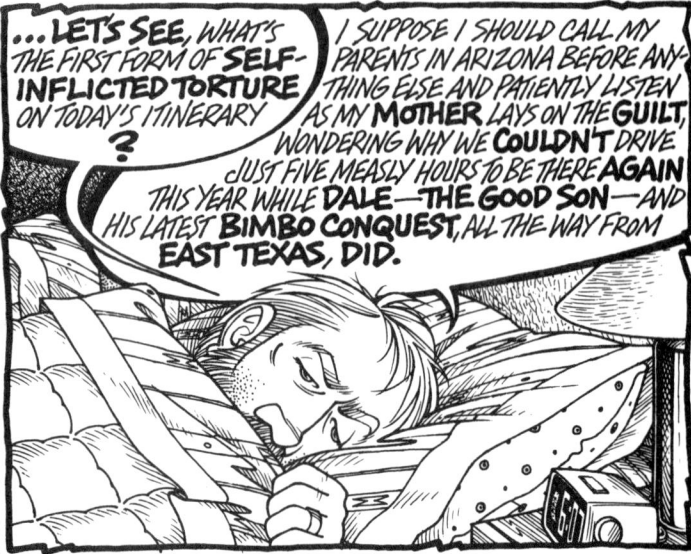

...LET'S SEE, WHAT'S THE FIRST FORM OF **SELF-INFLICTED TORTURE** ON TODAY'S ITINERARY?

I SUPPOSE I SHOULD CALL MY PARENTS IN ARIZONA BEFORE ANYTHING ELSE AND PATIENTLY LISTEN AS MY **MOTHER** LAYS ON THE **GUILT**, WONDERING WHY WE **COULDN'T** DRIVE JUST FIVE MEASLY HOURS TO BE THERE **AGAIN** THIS YEAR WHILE **DALE** —THE **GOOD SON**— AND HIS LATEST **BIMBO CONQUEST**, ALL THE WAY FROM **EAST TEXAS**, DID.

...AFTER BREAKFAST, I GUESS THE NEXT THING TO DO IS FINISH WRAPPING LAUREN'S GIFTS, ALL THOSE **EXPENSIVE** TOYS THAT SHE NEEDS LIKE A MANUAL ON **GRANDFATHER EXTORTION!**

AND I HAVE TO BE SURE THAT HER PRESENTS ARE **PROPERLY MARKED** THIS YEAR. I DON'T THINK I'LL **EVER** LIVE DOWN WHAT HAPPENED **LAST YEAR:** ALL THE GRANDPARENTS GATHERED AROUND THE TREE, CAMCORDERS BUZZING AS LAUREN TORE INTO THAT PACKAGE AND PULLED OUT A **STUDDED LEATHER JOCK STRAP.**

...AT LEAST **FRANK** APPRECIATED THE **BARBIE DOLL**... WE HAVE TO REMEMBER TO LEAVE EARLY AND STOP AT BOB AND FRANK'S FOR DRINKS AND HORS D'OEUVRES IN LONG BEACH BEFORE WE HEAD ON INTO ANAHEIM FOR THE REST OF OUR ANNUAL YULE TIDE **STUFFING AND MARINATING.**

I CAN'T REMEMBER...DO WE ACTUALLY EAT DINNER WITH MY EX AND RICHARD AND DEBBIE AND HER PARENTS THIS YEAR OR IS THAT **NEXT YEAR** AND **THIS YEAR** WE EAT WITH DAVID AND COLLIN AND **HIS FOLKS** AND JUST STOP AND VISIT AND EAT A **MEAL'S WORTH** OF CANDY, SNACKS AND JUNK WITH...BEFORE WE **ACTUALLY** GO TO DINNER AT...OR DO WE STOP AFTER ...OR IS THAT...OR DO WE...?

JIM BARELA

IF YOU'RE LOOKING FOR **SYMPATHY**, DON'T LOOK AT ME; I'M JEWISH.

ON BEHALF OF THE **ETHNICLY, CULTURALLY** AND **RELIGIOUSLY** DISADVANTAGED EVERYWHERE, MAY I JUST SAY, **THANKS FOR NOTHING!!**

...YA MEAN, THIS FELLA 'N' THIS FELLA?

YEAH.

AND THEY'VE BOTH BEEN DEAD A HUNDRED YEARS BUT, SOMETIMES, THEY COME 'N' VISIT YOU IN YER DREAMS 'N' TALK TO YA... AND YOU TALK TA THEM?

YEAH.

WEIRD!

OF COURSE, IN LIFE, THEY REALLY HATED EACH OTHER, SO MOSTLY THEY JUST BICKER AND TOSS INSULTS BACK AND FORTH. AND TCHAIKOVSKY WAS GAY; HE WAS CLOSETED AND LEAD A MISERABLE LIFE. IN DEATH, THOUGH, I IMAGINE HIM OUT— REALLY OUT. IN FACT, HE'S KIND OF...FLAMBOYANT. THE LAST TIME I SAW HIM WAS THE NIGHT WE FINALLY GOT TOGETHER. HE, SORT OF, GAVE OUR RELATIONSHIP HIS BLESSING.

REALLY WEIRD!

WELL, THEY'RE JUST FIGMENTS OF MY IMAGINATION, PRODUCTS OF MY SUBCONSCIOUS, MY FACINATION FOR TWO FAMOUS PEOPLE I ADMIRE...YOU KNOW.

NO. I DON'T.

AWW, C'MON! I KNOW THAT YOU JUST STUMBLED INTO THIS SHOW BUSINESS/MODELING/B-MOVIE CAREER THAT YOU'VE BEEN PERSUING SINCE YOU CAME TO CALIFORNIA. BUT YOU DO IT SO WELL! YOU MUST'VE HAD SOME KIND OF A ROLE MODEL, SOME FAMOUS PERSONALITY WHO YOU LOOKED UP TO, WHO YOU WANTED TO GROW UP TO BE LIKE— IT'S THE SAME KIND OF THING.

WELL,...

C'MON, THIS IS TRUE CONFESSIONS NIGHT! SPILL IT!

—SIGH— WHEN I WAS JUST A LITTLE KID—I MEAN A REAL LITTLE KID, JUST FOUR OR FIVE YEARS OLD —I WANTED MORE THAN ANYTHIN' IN THE WHOLE WORLD TA GROW UP TA BE PATSY CLINE.

YOU WHAT?! PATSY...?

CLINE. YUP, AND WHY NOT? SHE WAS ALWAYS MY FAVORITE COUNTRY STAR. SHE WAS SO BEAUTIFUL 'N' SANG SO PRETTY...

...MY FOLKS USED TA THINK IT WAS SO CUTE WHEN ONE OF HER SONGS WOULD COME ON THE RADIO AND I'D STAND THERE IN THE LIVIN' ROOM LIP SYNCIN' 'N' SWISHIN' ALL THOSE IMAGINARY PETTICOATS, CURTSYIN' TA THE IMAGINARY APPLAUSE OF MY HUNDREDS OF ADORIN' FANS... SHIT! ALL THAT TIME AGO 'N' I WAS ALREADY SHOWIN' MY PINK!

O' COURSE, AS I GOT OLDER, MY MAMA WOULD SAY, "MERLE, YOU STOP THAT, NOW, OR YOU'RE GONNA GROW UP TA BE A SISSY!"

JIM BARELA

...SO I DID... AND I GREW UP TA BE A SISSY, ANYWAY!

AND, IF YOUR MOTHER COULD ONLY SEE WHAT AN EXCELLENT JOB YOU'RE DOING, SHE'D BE SO PROUD!

YOU'VE GOT CAPPUCCINO FROTH ALL OVER YOUR MUSTACHE, SWEETUMS —LET ME GET IT.

AWW THANK YOU, HONEY BEAR.

GEEZ! AND WE ALL JUST ATE!

LARRY!... SO, TELL US ALL ABOUT THE REST OF YOUR WEEKEND IN LAS VEGAS. YOU SAID THAT SOMETHING ELSE REALLY SPECIAL HAPPENED. WHAT WAS IT?

WELL, YA SEE, I HAVE THIS FRIEND, HECTOR HERNANDEZ. HE'S A MEMBER OF "THE TRIBE" 'N' ALL; I MET 'IM AT ONE O' MY CASTIN' CALLS. HECTOR'S 'N ELVIS IMPERSONATOR...

ANYWAY, HE GOT A GIG WORKIN' ONE O' THOSE 24 HOUR, QUICKIE WEDDIN' CHAPELS IN VEGAS AND WE WENT TA VISIT 'IM ONE NIGHT...

A GAY ELVIS IMPERSONATOR?

...WELL, IT TURNS OUT THAT 'EVER'BODY AT THAT WEDDIN' CHAPEL IS QUEER, FROM THE MINISTER RIGHT ON DOWN TO THE LIL' OL' DYKE WHO PLAYED THE TAPE RECORDED WEDDIN' MARCH. ANYWAY, IT BEIN' A SLOW EVENIN' 'N' ALL....AWW, YOU TELL 'EM, JIM.

HECTOR TOLD THEM ALL ABOUT US. HOW WE JUST GOT TOGETHER, HOW WE'RE IN LOVE 'N' ALL....WELL, THEY TALKED US INTO IT...WE DIDN'T JUST GET RINGS, WE, SORT OF, GOT MARRIED. IT WAS THE MOST WONDERFUL, ROMANTIC THING I'VE EVER DONE. HECTOR EVEN SANG "LOVE ME TENDER" JUST FOR US.

OH HOW GREAT! OH CONGRATULATIONS, YOU GUYS! OH LARRY, ISN'T IT WONDERFUL?! OH ... WE SHOULD DO THAT SOME DAY, YOU KNOW.

WHAT? HIRE A GAY ELVIS IMPERSONATOR?

NO, NO! YOU KNOW, MAKE IT OFFICIAL: HAVE A LITTLE CEREMONY WITH OUR DEAREST FRIENDS, EXCHANGE VOWS... WE COULD HAVE IT IN THE SPRING FOR OUR FOURTEENTH ANNIVERSARY; I KNOW THIS LESBIAN RABBI; WE COULD SET UP THE CHUPA IN THE BACK YARD, ON THE PATIO NEXT TO THE ORANGE TREE; I HOPE IT'S STILL IN BLOOM BY THE TIME WE....

HOLD IT! TIME OUT! DON'T YOU THINK THAT IT WOULD BE A GOOD IDEA TO CONSULT THE GROOM FIRST? I MEAN, I'M HAPPY FOR JIM 'N' MERLE 'N' ALL, BUT US? OUT IN THE YARD WITH A RABBI, OUR FRIENDS AND ALL OUR NOSEY NEIGHBORS, NO LESS? GET REAL, LEONARD! DON'T BE SILLY!

I'M NOT BEING "SILLY", I'M TOTALLY SERIOUS. YOU KNOW THAT I'VE BEEN WANTING US TO DO SOMETHING LIKE THIS FOR QUITE SOME TIME NOW; IT'S VERY IMPORTANT TO ME. OF COURSE, IF CERTAIN PEOPLE CAN'T SEE THAT, PERHAPS OUR RELATIONSHIP JUST ISN'T VERY IMPORTANT TO THEM ANYMORE.

UUGGGH!! IT'S GOING TO BE A LONG, LONG NIGHT!

GO AHEAD. GO AHEAD 'N' TRY TA GET THE WEEKEND OFF AGAIN ANYTIME SOON. ANYTIME BETWEEN NOW AND WHEN HELL FREEZES OVER!!

JIM BARELA

SORRY I'M LATE. I'M HAPPY, THOUGH, TO SEE THAT BRUNO WAS SWEET ENOUGH TO KEEP COMPANY WITH YOU UNTIL I WAS ABLE TO JOIN THE PARTY—WORTHLESS BASTARD!
...MY, AREN'T WE STUNNING TONIGHT! I MUST SAY THAT THIS IS THE FIRST TIME ANY BURGLER BROKE INTO MY HOUSE WEARING A BLACK EVENING GOWN. BUT THEN, I KNEW IT WAS YOU SO, SOMEHOW, I'M NOT SURPRISED.
HOW DID YOU KNOW THAT IT WAS ME?
A REAL BURGLER WOULDN'T TRY TO LOOK FOR THE FAMILY JEWELS AND ASSORTED VALUABLES INSIDE MY PIANO. WHEN I HEARD THE LID COME CRASHING DOWN WITH THAT GIANT "EL CABONG!" SOUND, I THOUGHT, WHO ELSE COULD IT BE?
ARE YOU GOING TO CALL THE POLICE?
CLICK
IT'S A DONE DEAL, DEAR. LONG BEACH'S FINEST SHOULD BE HERE ANY MINUTE NOW TO BRING YOUR CELEBRITY STALKING CAREER TO IT'S LONG ANTICIPATED END. THANKS FOR DROPPING BY AND HELPING ME MAKE IT ALL POSSIBLE.
OH, I'M SO ASHAMED! I'VE ACTUALLY ALLOWED MY MANIC OBSESSION FOR MOZART TO BRING ME TO THIS: A LIFE OF CRIME! WHAT AN AWFUL WAY TO REPAY THIS LOVELY MAN, THIS GENIUS WHO PLAYS THE TWENTY FIRST CONCERTO MORE BEAUTIFULLY THAN ANYONE I'VE EVER HEARD, A MAN WHO BROUGHT SUCH UTTER JOY TO MY LONELY, LOVELESS EXISTANCE WITH HIS LITTLE C.D.—
...HOW FOOLISH IT WAS FOR ME TO THINK, BY BREAKING INTO HIS HOME, THAT, SOMEHOW, I COULD FULFILL ONE OF MY FONDEST FANTASIES, THAT HE WOULD ACTUALLY CONSENT TO SIT HERE NEXT TO ME AT HIS OWN PIANO AND PLAY —JUST FOR ME— THE SLOW MOVEMENT OF "EINE KLEINE NACHTMUSIK". OH, FOR JUST THAT SWEET, RARE PRIVILEGE, I'D GLADLY GO WITH THE POLICE, SATISFIED AND PROMISING TO NEVER BOTHER HIM EVER AGAIN.
IS THAT REALLY ALL THAT YOU WANT?
OH YES, MR. MENDEZ!
AND, WHEN THE POLICE COME, YOU WON'T TELL THEM THAT YOU'RE MY WIFE OR SISTER OR SOME LONG LOST, LOONY RELATIVE?
I PROMISE!
WELL...
OH, AND IF YOU COULD SLIP OFF YOUR BATHROBE AND DO IT IN THE NUDE—THAT'S A BIG PART OF MY FANTASY, TOO.
FRANK, CALL 911 AGAIN AND TELL THEM TO MOVE THEIR BUTTS!!
JIM BARELA

...AND TO THINK, ALL ALONG I HAD ASSUMED THAT SHE WAS NOTHING MORE THAN A **FIGMENT** OF BOB'S **IMAGINATION.** YET, THERE SHE WAS, LITERALLY **BIGGER THAN LIFE,** SITTING AT BOB'S PIANO IN A BLACK, SEQUINED EVENING GOWN—A GARDENIA IN HER HAIR, NO LESS—A REAL, LIVE CELEBRITY **STALKER** IN OUR LIVING ROOM, IN THE MIDDLE OF THE NIGHT?... TALK ABOUT **CREEPY;** MAN, WAS I GLAD TO SEE THE **POLICE!** OF COURSE, **BRUNO THE WONDER DOG** TRIED TO **ATTACK THEM** AS THEY HAULED HER OFF TO THEIR PATROL CAR...

...THIS PLACE REMINDS ME OF THAT "**B**" GRADE **SLASHER** MOVIE, "**SLAY RIDE**", STARRING YOUR FRIEND, **MERLE,** AND **LARRY'S BROTHER'S** OLD GIRLFRIEND AS THE NEWLYWED COUPLE **LOST** IN THE **SNOWY WOODS** WHERE THE **HOMICIDAL MANIAC** WITH THE **AX** COULD BE HIDING BEHIND ANY... BY THE WAY, YOU DO REMEMBER WHERE WE **PARKED** THE CAR, **DON'T YOU?**

IT'S **RIGHT UP** THERE ON THE HIGHWAY, BOB. WE'RE **SO** CLOSE YOU CAN **HEAR** THE TRAFFIC.

ANYWAY, LAST MONTH WAS MY **FIRST** EXPERIENCE HOSTING A **STALKER** AS WELL AS FRANK'S **UNIFORM CLUB** IN OUR HOME, AND I HONESTLY **CAN'T** SAY **WHICH** MADE A MORE LASTING IMPRESSION. HOWEVER, THE LATTER ALL A-TWITTER OVER GETTING **MACHO** AT SOMETHING CALLED A "**SOLDIER OF FORTUNE WEEKEND**" —"WE CAN ALL WEAR OUR **CAMMIES!**"—WAS TRULY A **SPECIAL MOMENT.**

WELL, **FRANK** WILL BE PERFECTLY WELCOME TO WEAR HIS "**CAMMIES**" OR HIS UNIFORM OR WHATEVER. **LARRY AND I** WILL BE WEARING MATCHING PEARL GRAY **TUXEDOS** AS WE STAND THERE UNDER THE **CHUPA** WITH THE RABBI, EXCHANGING **VOWS** IN THE GARDEN, LATE IN THE WARM AFTERNOON OF THAT BEAUTIFUL DAY IN SPRING.

OH HOW **CUTE!** WHAT'S THAT ALL ABOUT?

IT'S ABOUT TAKING EVERY OPPORTUNITY TO MAKE MY LIFE A COMPLETE **LIVING HELL!** LEONARD HAS THIS FANTASY ABOUT THE TWO OF US GETTING "**MARRIED**" FOR OUR FOURTEENTH ANNIVERSARY—IT'S **ONLY A FANTASY**...GIVE IT A REST, DEAR.

TIM BARELA

OH, BUT THERE'S **NO TIME** TO REST, DEAR. IT'S ALMOST **SPRING.** THERE ARE LOTS OF DETAILS TO ATTEND TO BEFORE THE **BIG DAY:** A MENU TO DECIDE ON, A GUEST LIST TO COMPILE... I'VE ALREADY SPOKEN TO THE **RABBI** AND THE **CATERER** AND THE **PRINTER**—ALL THE INVITATIONS WILL BE ENGRAVED, OF COURSE; **YOU'LL** BE GETTING ONE LIKE EVERYBODY ELSE. THERE'LL BE AN **R.S.V.P.** NUMBER AND THE REST WILL BE COMPLETELY UP TO **YOU** AT THAT POINT. WE **TRULY** HOPE THAT YOU'LL BE ABLE TO **JOIN US...**

...BECAUSE, IF THE **GROOM** DECIDES NOT TO...

UGGGH! THAT'S WHAT HAPPENED TO THAT **JERK** SKI INSTRUCTOR IN THE MOVIE, IN THE DESERTED **LODGE!!**

WHY DOES THE WORD, "**BOBBITT**" SUDDENLY SPRING TO MIND?

UH-OH, I KNOW THAT **DAZED** LOOK. STOOD IN LINE ALL DAY AT THE LATEST CASTING CALL FOR NOTHING **AGAIN**, HUH?

...WELL, DON'T WORRY, HON. WE'LL JUST HAVE TO SAVE A LITTLE LONGER FOR THE FIRST AND LAST MONTH'S ON THAT LITTLE HOUSE WE WANT, THAT'S ALL.

I GOT THE PART.

I GOT THE PART!

I'VE GOT THE SCRIPT, RIGHT HERE. I GO IN FER WARDROBE 'N' MAKE-UP TESTS 'N' SUCH, TAMARRA...

WHAT?

YOU GOT IT? YOU **REALLY** GOT IT?!

...ME, MERLE OBERON FROM TYLERVILLE, TEXAS! ME, AS THE BRAND NEW CHARACTER IN A **TOP**-RATED, PRIME TIME NETWORK SITCOM!!

BUT HOW?... WHO?...

BERNIE GOLDMAN—LEONARD'S **BROTHER**—THAT'S WHO. HE REMEMBERED ME FROM LAST SUMMER, AT LARRY'S BIRTHDAY PARTY WHERE I MET **YOU**. BERNIE'S ONE O' THE **STAFF WRITERS** FER THE SHOW. HE STOPPED TA SAY "HI" WHEN HE SAW ME WAITIN' IN LINE AND THE NEXT THING I KNOW I'M GETTIN' CALLED IN TA SEE THE CASTIN' DIRECTOR 'N' THE PRODUCER **BEFORE** JUST ABOUT **ANYBODY** ELSE—AND I GOT THE PART! ...I SURE AM GLAD THAT I WENT TA **THAT** PARTY!

I GET TA PLAY **JAKE**, "THE **SEXY** RANCH HAND", BY THE WAY.

"RANCH HAND"? THIS SHOW DOESN'T HAVE A **RANCH**; IT TAKES PLACE IN CHICAGO.

RIGHT. IT ALL HAS TA DO WITH THIS MAJOR, END-OF-SEASON **PLOT-TWIST** THAT BERNIE AND THE OTHER WRITERS CAME UP WITH. YA SEE, ONE O' THE MAIN CHARACTERS HAS A RICH OL' UNCLE WHO DIES 'N' SHE INHERITS THIS RANCH IN WYOMIN' 'N'...

WYOMING?...SWEETHEART, I'M HAPPY FOR YOU AND ALL, I'M HAPPY FOR US—CONGRATULATIONS!....BUT WYOMING? YOU'LL HAVE TO GO AWAY TO WYOMING?

AW, HONEY BEAR, NO; I'M **NOT** GOIN' NOWHERE! THIS IS HOLLYWOOD. THEY DON'T SHOOT THE REST OF THE TV SHOW IN CHICAGO, THEY DO ALL THAT IN **BURBANK.**

...AND ALL THE **WYOMIN'** STUFF'LL BE DONE OUT IN **SIMI VALLEY.** THE SET IS AT THE STUDIO'S "MOVIE RANCH", JUST UP THE ROAD FROM THE **JUSTICE CENTER**—YA KNOW, WHERE THE COURTHOUSE IS—AND JUST OVER THE HILL FROM THE **REAGAN PRESIDENTIAL LIBRARY.**

AH YES, THE LOVELY SIMI VALLEY: LAND OF **MAKE BELIEVE.**

JIM BARELA

...HEY, IT'S GONNA BE **GREAT!** **TRUST ME,** BY THE END OF THE SEASON, HALF OF THE WOMEN AND A FAIR NUMBER OF THE **MEN** IN THIS COUNTRY WILL BE TUNING IN EACH WEEK TO **DROOL** OVER JAKE, "THE **SEXY** RANCH HAND"—THAT GUY'S A **NATURAL!**...

...YEAH. I JUST WISH THAT THEY HADN'T FINISHED RE-BUILDING THE SETS SO SOON; PRODUCTION COULDN'T'VE STARTED UP AGAIN, FOR ME, AT A **WORSE TIME!**...YEAH, MY LIFE IS IN CHAOS! IT'S A TOTAL **MADHOUSE** HERE!

...**NO,** NO WAY! THEY JUST FINISHED FIXING MY PLACE IN WOODLAND HILLS, BUT THEY'RE STILL **PAINTING**—YOU KNOW MY **ALERGIES.** SO I'M NOT THERE, I'M SPENDING A FEW DAYS AT MY BROTHER'S PLACE AND IT'S A TOTAL **MADHOUSE** HERE!

...**MY MOTHER?** **SURE,** I COULD'VE GONE TO STAY WITH MY MOTHER, INSTEAD. I ALSO COULD'VE SHOVED **SEWING NEEDLES** IN MY **EYEBALLS!** I'LL TAKE THE MADHOUSE, THANK YOU.

...**WELL,** THIS WEEKEND, THEY HAVE A BUNCH OF GUYS HERE FINALLY FIXING THEIR **QUAKE DAMAGE**... **NAW,** NOTHING MAJOR OR STRUCTURAL OR ANYTHING LIKE THAT, JUST A LOT OF CRACKED PLASTER 'N' STUFF...

...YEAH, AND ON TOP OF EVERYTHING ELSE, THIS IS THE WEEKEND THAT MY BROTHER'S LOVER'S KID AND HIS ROOMMATE ARE MOVING OUT **AGAIN.** CAN YOU BELIEVE IT? THE KID JUST STARTED AT CAL STATE **NORTHRIDGE** A FEW MONTHS AGO; THIER ORIGINAL OFF-CAMPUS APART-MENT IS **ANCIENT HISTORY.**

...THAT'S RIGHT, MY BROTHER'S **GAY.** ...**NAW,** HE DOSEN'T CARE WHO KNOWS. **IN FACT,** I'LL CLUE YA IN AS TO WHY THEY'RE IN SUCH A RUSH TO GET THIS PLACE BACK IN **SHIP SHAPE:** MY BROTHER AND HIS **BALL 'N' CHAIN,** AFTER FOURTEEN YEARS TOGETHER THEY'RE FINALLY MAKING IT **OFFICIAL.** THEY'RE GET-TING **MARRIED!**...

...YEAH, AIN'T THAT A **KICK?!**...YEAH, IN A FEW WEEKS, IN THE BACK YARD WITH A RABBI 'N' **EVERYTHING;** I'M NOT GONNA MISS IT **FOR THE WORLD!** IT'S GONNA BE ONE **BIG SHINDIG,** A HOUSE FULL OF PEOPLE AND FOOD COMING OUT OF YOUR **EARS!**

...YOU BET. IN FACT, MY BROTHER AND THE **CATERER** ARE SITTING AT THE DINING ROOM TABLE, **RIGHT NOW,** DECIDING ON A **COLOR SCEME** FOR THE **BUFFET**...

...**NO,** IT'S NOT WIERD, I THINK IT'S **GREAT!** IN FACT, I THINK IT HAS **POTENTIAL.** ...**RIGHT!** A LITTLE CREA-TIVE WRITING HERE, A LITTLE POETIC LICENSE THERE AND WE COULD GET **TWO,** MAYBE **THREE** EPISODES OF THE SHOW, NEXT SEASON, OUT OF ALL THIS!

IF YOU ASK ME, THE APRICOT AND **TEAL** COMBINATION **IS** JUST A BIT MUCH. IF I WERE YOU, I'D GO WITH SOMETHING SIMPLE YET **TASTEFUL**... LIKE **PEACH** OR PERHAPS A NICE **MAUVE.**

I DIDN'T HIRE YOU FOR YOUR OPINION; SHUT-UP 'N' **SPACKLE!** ...DAMN GAY YELLOW PAGES!

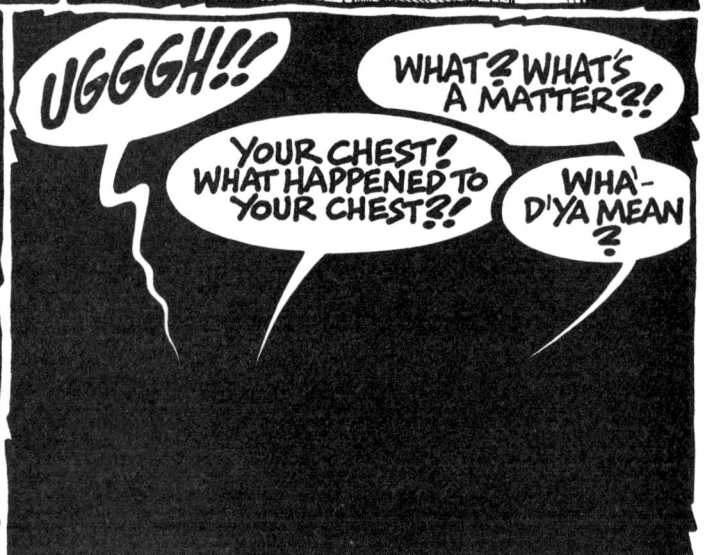

38

LAST YEAR, I THOUGHT THAT I'D FINALLY SEEN THE LAST OF DAVID'S THINGS AND I'D HAVE THE SPARE BEDROOM TO MYSELF... LITTLE DID I KNOW THAT MOST OF IT WOULD RETURN IN A MERE MATTER OF MONTHS TO BE HELD IN STORAGE.

BUT NOW—HAPPY DAY! —I CAN HAVE THE SEWING ROOM THAT I'VE ALWAYS WANTED... NOW ALL I HAVE TO DO IS GET A SEWING MACHINE AND LEARN HOW TO USE IT.

EARTHQUAKES HAVE NO APPRECIATION FOR HOBBIES... WELL, THIS SHOULD BE THE LAST OF IT.

...IT'S OFF TO DAVID AND COLLIN'S NEW PLACE IN THE VALLEY FOR ME. I JUST HOPE THE TRAFFIC'S BETTER; LEONARD'S GONNA BE PISSED IF I DON'T MAKE IT HOME BY DAWN.

BY THE WAY, I WILL R.S.V.P. OFFICIALLY, BUT GO AHEAD AND TELL LEONARD THAT I'LL DEFFINATELY BE THERE ON THE FOURTEENTH. YOU KNOW, AT THE WEDDING.

AW, FER CHRISSAKES, SHARON! HE DIDN'T INVITE YOU TA THAT ABOMINABLE MISHEGAS, TOO? SHIT!!

OF COURSE HE DID. OUR ONLY GRANDDAUGHTER IS GOING TO BE THE FLOWER GIRL. IT MAY NOT BE EXACTLY THE KIND OF CERIMONY I'D ALWAYS PICTURED, BUT I'M NOT MISSING IT FOR THE WORLD!

THERE MAY NOT BE A CERIMONY —OF ANY KIND. I SWORE, UP AND DOWN, THAT I WOULD NEVER WILLINGLY PUT MYSELF THRU ANYTHING THAT HORRIFIC EVER AGAIN AND I MEANT IT!

ARE YOU, BY CHANCE, REFERING TO OUR WEDDING?

YOU MEAN "THE WEDDING FROM HELL"? OF COURSE I AM! THERE WE WERE, NOT A YEAR OUT OF HIGH SCHOOL, THE SWORD OF THE VIETNAM WAR AND THE DRAFT LOTTERY HANGING OVER MY HEAD. YOUR PARENTS HATED ME, YOUR BROTHERS HATED ME, ALL YOUR OBNOXIOUS RELATIVES HATED ME. IF YOU HAVE ANY DOUBTS AS TO THE HELLACIOUSNESS OF THAT DAY, JUST CHECK OUT THE PHOTOS: ME AND MY FRIENDS IN THOSE LIME GREEN TUXEDOS WITH THE BELL-BOTTOMS AND PINK RUFFLED SHIRTS; YOUR FRIENDS—WHO HATED ME— IN THOSE HIDEOUS PURPLE, ORANGE AND AVOCADO BRIDE'S MAIDS DRESSES.

LARRY, THIS IS 1994, NOT 1971. WE'RE ALL OLDER AND, HOPEFULLY, HAVE A MORE MATURE SENSE OF STYLE AND GOOD TASTE...

OH YEAH? DID I TELL YOU ABOUT LEONARD'S APRICOT AND TEAL BUFFET?

...AND THERE ARE PLENTY OF OTHER SIGNIFICANT DIFFERENCES BETWEEN THEN AND NOW, NOT THE LEAST OF WHICH CONCERNS THE PESKY LITTLE FACT THAT —UNLIKE US, TWENTY-THREE YEARS AGO—LEONARD AND YOU REALLY DO LOVE EACH OTHER.

I DON'T KNOW HOW HE PUTS UP WITH YOU—I COULDN'T. THAT LEONARD WOULD DO ALL THIS PLANNING 'N' PRERARATION FOR THE LOVE OF YOU IS AS AMAZING AS IT IS ENDEARING. AND IF YOU DON'T GO THRU WITH IT FOR HIM, IF NOT YOURSELF...WELL, YOU REALLY ARE AS STUPID AS MY MOTHER ALWAYS SAID YOU WERE.

...BESIDES, I'M REALLY LOOKING FORWARD TO THIS. I'M OVER FORTY, I'VE BEEN DIVORCED FOR FOURTEEN YEARS AND I'M STILL SINGLE. THESE DAYS, I'LL GO TO JUST ABOUT ANYTHING WHERE I'LL HAVE HALF A CHANCE OF CATCHING THE BOUQUET!

I'LL BE SURE TO HAVE LEONARD SET YOU IN HIS SIGHTS. ...READY, AIM, FIRE!...

TIM BARELA

LEONARD?... ...LEONARD, WHAT ARE YOU DOING OUT THERE AT ONE O'CLOCK IN THE MORNING?

KILLING SNAILS. I COULDN'T SLEEP, SO I CAME OUT HERE TO SIT FOR A WHILE AND FOUND SNAILS ALL OVER YOUR BROCCOLI PLANTS.

YOU'VE BEEN KILLING SNAILS?

SURE IT'S A PIECE O' CAKE. I JUST IMAGINE THAT THEIR SHELLS ARE THE FACE OF A CERTAIN SOMEONE THEN I MASH THEIR SLIMY LITTLE BODIES INTO THE GROUND.

WELL, THIS IS WHY THEY'RE ALL OVER THE PLACE: THEY'RE ALL OUT OF BEER... SEE? THE BOTTLE'S HERE, UNDER THIS CABBAGE.

"OUT OF BEER"? YOU GIVE SNAILS BEER? I THOUGHT THAT YOU WERE FEEDING THE CAT FROM NEXT DOOR WITH THAT DISH.

NO, LEONARD, THE DISH AND THE BEER ARE FOR THE SNAILS. SNAILS LOVE BEER. IN FACT, THEY LOVE IT SO MUCH, THEY'LL DROWN THEMSELVES IN IT.

GOSH, TO LOVE SOMETHING SO MUCH THAT YOU'RE WILLING TO DROWN YOURSELF IN IT. ...I THINK I KNOW HOW THEY FEEL.

LEONARD,....I'VE BEEN THINKING...YA KNOW, ABOUT US, ABOUT THE WEDDING, ABOUT ALL THOSE THINGS YOU SAID... MAYBE I HAVE BEEN KIND'VE "NEGATIVE" ABOUT A LOT OF DIFFERENT THINGS, LATELY. MAYBE I HAVE GROWN "COMPLACENT" ABOUT THE INFORMALITY OF OUR RELATIONSHIP: NO PAPERS, NO CEREMONIES, NO "REAL PROMISES". LIKE A LOT OF OTHER GUYS—NO MUSS, NO FUSS; IT'S BEEN GREAT, BUT, IF AND WHEN YOU HAVE TO, YOU'RE FREE TO JUST CALL IT QUITS.

...WELL, IF, SOMEDAY, I DID DECIDE TO "JUST WALK OUT"...WHERE WOULD I GO?

...LEONARD JACOB GOLDMAN, MAN THAT I LOVE, THE ONLY MAN THAT I'VE EVER REALLY LOVED IN MY ENTIRE STUPID, SELFISH LIFE, WHICH WOULD BE SO EMPTY AND LOST WITHOUT YOU IN IT...LEONARD, WILL YOU MARRY ME?

WELL, I'LL THINK ABOUT IT...

FINE... BUT JUST HURRY, WOULD YA? I'M KNEELING ON A SNAIL AND IT'S STARTING TO OOZE THRU MY PANTS.

...OK.

JIM BREZA

41

Panel 1:

LEONARD, JUST **HOW MANY** TIMES ARE YOU GOING TO HAVE TO WATCH THAT **DAMN** VIDEO BEFORE YOU GROW AS **TIRED** OF SEEING IT **AS I AM?**

THIS IS THE VIDEO OF THE **HAPPIEST DAY** OF MY LIFE; I DON'T THINK I'LL **EVER** GET TIRED OF SEEING IT.

OH JOY. ...THEN I GUESS I'LL NEVER GET TO USE IT TO RECORD RERUNS OF "**REN & STIMPY.**"

Panel 2:

DO IT AND I'LL FEED YOUR BALLS TO THE SNAILS!

...OH **LOOK,** THERE'S YOUR KIDS, THEIR **MOM 'N' SPOUSES**...ISN'T THE **FLOWER GIRL** JUST **ADORABLE?!**

HEY, WHAT CAN I SAY? I PASS ALONG **GREAT GENETIC MATERIAL.**

Panel 3:

...AND THERE'S MY BROTHER WITH YOUR MOM AND MY PARENTS. IT WAS **TRULY FRIGHTENING** HOW **WELL** YOUR MOTHER AND MY MOTHER **GOT ALONG TOGETHER.**

FOR A THREE-YEAR-OLD, THAT FLOWER GIRL **REALLY** KNEW HOW TO WORK THE CROWD LIKE A **PRO.**

PARENTS ARE **SUCKERS** FOR CUTENESS AND GREAT GRANDCHILDREN **INSTINCTIVELY** KNOW HOW TO **EXPLOIT** IT.

Panel 4:

BOB PLAYED BEAUTIFULLY ON THAT **RINKY-DINK,** RENTED ELECTRIC KEYBOARD.

JIM WAS SO EXCITED TO MEET A REAL CONCERT PIANIST. ALMOST AS EXCITED AS FRANK WAS TO MEET A **REAL, LIVE TV STAR.**

IT'S HARD TO BELIEVE THAT, AFTER JUST A FEW WEEK'S ON YOUR BROTHER'S **CRUMMY** SIT-COM, MERLE'S BECOME SO **POPULAR** WITH THE AUDIENCE THAT **TV GUIDE** USED A PHOTO OF HIS CO-STAR **WITH HIM** ON THEIR COVER.

SEX SELLS.

Panel 5:

AWWW, AND THERE WE ARE...NOW, THAT WASN'T SO BAD, WAS IT?

NO, IT WASN'T. IN FACT, IT WAS **WONDERFUL** AND I'D DO IT **AGAIN** IN A FLASH!

Panel 6:

AND THERE'S **HECTOR**... I MUST SAY, HAVING A CHUBBY, GAY, CHICANO **ELVIS IMPERSONATOR** IN A WHITE, RHINESTONED JUMP SUIT, WITH A BELT BUCKLE THE SIZE OF A **TEXAS LICENSE PLATE,** SINGING "THE HAWAIIAN WEDDING SONG" CERTAINLY DID ADD AN...**UNEXPECTED DIMENSION** TO OUR LITTLE AFTERNOON.

YOU MEAN, **TOOK** THE AFTERNOON **INTO** AN UNEXPECTED DIMENSION! ...I REALLY WISH THAT JIM AND MERLE HAD JUST GIVEN US A **BLENDER,** INSTEAD.

JIM BARELA

WELL, THERE'S JIM 'N' THE TRUCK, COME TA FETCH ME.

BY THE WAY, JUST WHAT WERE YOU AND THE LIGHTING DIRECTOR LAUGHING ABOUT DURING THAT LAST SCENE OF MINE?

AW, NOTHIN'. JUST ABOUT ALL THIS HOLLYWOOD STUFF, I GUESS...

...I MEAN, HERE WE ARE IN THE SIMI VALLEY, PERTENDIN' THAT WE'RE REALLY OUT IN WYOMIN', 'N' THERE YOU WERE, LOOKIN' AT THE SANTA SUSANA MOUNTAINS 'N' SAYIN' ALL THAT STUFF ABOUT "THE MAJESTIC GRAND TETONS"!...I WAS JUST TELLIN' RUSS THAT "GRAND TETONS" TRANSLATES TA "BIG TITS"—THOSE EARLY FRENCH TRAPPERS MUST'VE BEEN REALLY LONELY!—I'M HALF FRENCH, I SHOULD KNOW.

ABOUT BEING LONELY?

HOLLYWOOD CATERING

NO, 'BOUT KINDA KNOWIN' HOW TA SPEEK FRENCH. YA KNOW, PARLEZ-VOUS ESCARGO? 'N' SUCH.

MERLE, ARE YOU GOING TO MISS ME? I MEAN, OVER "HIATUS." IT'S GOING TO BE MONTHS BEFORE WE GET TO WORK TOGETHER AGAIN.

WELL, YEAH, BUT WE'LL BE DOIN' LOTS O' STUFF TOGETHER THIS SUMMER, LIKE THAT INTERVIEW WITH SAM RUBIN ON THE CHANNEL FIVE MORNIN' NEWS NEXT WEEK.

...WELL, I'M GOING TO MISS YOU. AND, YA KNOW, THE BIG STUFF THAT I HAVE ISN'T MADE OF STONE.

ONE THING'S FOR SURE, THAT MUSTACHE OF YOUR'S SIMPLY HAS TO GO BEFORE WE START FILMING AGAIN NEXT SEASON; THE TOM SELLECK LOOK IS OUT! ....SEE YA NEXT WEEK.

G'BYE.

JIM BARELA

C'MON, BABE, LET'S GET ON HOME. I'M TIRED.

I'LL BET! THAT LOOKED ABSOLUTELY EXHAUSTING!!

43

...IT WAS 'N END O' SEASON/ "WRAP" PARTY GIFT. AREN'T YOU PROUD OF ME? I'VE JUST BEEN A PART O' THE SHOW FER A FEW MONTHS 'N' I'VE ALREADY BEEN ON THE COVER O' TV GUIDE!

OF COURSE I'M PROUD OF YOU. BUT THAT THING ISN'T SO MUCH A PICTURE OF YOU AS IT IS A PICTURE OF HER, AND I WILL NOT HAVE A PHOTOGRAPH OF THAT WOMAN HANGING FROM ANYTHING LESS THAN A NOOSE IN MY APARTMENT!

Sam & Jake TV'S HOT NEW ITEM

A PERSON WOULD THINK THAT YOU WERE ACTU'LY JEALOUS O' CINDY.

WELL, HOW DO YOU EXPECT ME TO FEEL? WHEN I MET YOU, A YEAR AGO, YOU WERE NOBODY. NOW, SUDDENLY, YOU'RE FAMOUS: THE HOT NEW CHARACTER ON A POPULAR SITCOM, YOUR PHOTO ON THE COVER OF TV GUIDE, ALL THE LATEST RUMORS ABOUT YOU AND YOUR CO-STAR SPLASHED ACROSS THE COVERS OF EVERY TABLOID IN THE SUPERMARKET!!

KITTY CHOW

Milk

OH, THAT... JIM, THE PUBLICITY PEOPLE AT THE PRODUCTION COMPANY DREAMED-UP THAT STORY ABOUT ME 'N' CINDY 'N' LEAKED IT TA THE TABLOIDS — IT'S GOOD FER RATIN'S.

"GOOD FOR RATINGS"? HOW SPECIAL! I'M SO HAPPY FOR THE NETWORK! IN THE MEAN TIME, IT WOULD SEEM THAT YOUR SWEET, SCHEMING LITTLE CO-WORKER IS AFTER MORE THAN JUST NUMBERS AND ADVERTISING REVENUE. I THINK THAT SHE'S STARTING TO BELIEVE HER OWN PUBLICITY!

AW, JIM, YOU'VE SEEN ME 'N' CINDY KISSIN' LOTS O' TIMES.

YEAH, ON TV. BUT I SAW NO CAMERAS, THE OTHER DAY. THAT WET, PASSIONATE PECK WAS FOR THE OBVIOUS BENEFIT OF AN AUDIENCE OF ONE AND THE MESSAGE WAS LOUD AND CLEAR!

WELL, LET ME MAKE THIS MESSAGE LOUD 'N' CLEAR: JIM, I LOVE YOU! CINDY IS NOTHIN' MORE TA ME THAN JUST ANOTHER "CO-WORKER". WHEN SHE KISSES ME I DON'T FEEL NOTHIN'. HELL, I USED TA HAVE SEX WITH WOMEN; A LITTLE KISS IS NO BIG DEAL!

JIM BARELA

SEX? YOU ACTUALLY USED TO HAVE SEX... WITH WOMEN?...EEEW!

WELL, SURE. I USED TA FORCE MYSELF TA DO LOTS O' DUMB THINGS TA PROVE TA MY FRIENDS — AND TA MYSELF — THAT I WASN'T QUEER.

YEAH, BUT TO ACTUALLY HAVE SEX WITH...EEEEWW!! GOSH, I'VE NEVER EVEN DONE THAT... WHAT WAS IT LIKE?

SORTA LIKE HAVIN' TA GO TA THE PRINCIPAL'S OFFICE, ONLY A LOT MORE UP CLOSE 'N' PERSONAL.

...WELL, I'VE HAD A WONDERFUL TIME; I DON'T SEE WHAT YOU HAVE TO COMPLAIN ABOUT, LARRY.

WELL, YEAH, I'VE HAD A NICE TIME, TOO. I JUST CAN'T SEE WHY, IF WE WERE GONNA SPEND THE LAST PART OF OUR "HONEYMOON" VACATION IN THE WINE COUNTRY, WE COULDN'T HAVE GONE TO NAPA. WHY, OF ALL PLACES, TEMECULA?

BECAUSE WE HAVEN'T SEEN ED AND MITCH IN AGES AND THEY OFFERED.

S&M CELLARS
WINE TASTING ROOM

...BESIDES, IF WE REALLY HAD HEADED UP NORTH, KNOWING YOU, WE WOULD'VE EVENTUALLY ENDED UP IN SAN FRANCISCO AND I WOULD'VE FOUND MYSELF COMPETING FOR YOUR ATTENTION WITH EVERY OTHER LEATHER CLAD CLONE ON CASTRO STREET? AT LEAST ALL THE COWBOYS THAT YOU'VE BEEN OGLING AROUND HERE ARE PRESUMABLY STRAIGHT AND OFF LIMITS.

OK, OK! SO MY EYES STILL WORK—SO SUE ME!...YES, IT HAS BEEN NICE TO SEE MITCH AND ED AGAIN. BUT, AS OF TODAY, WE'VE SEEN THEM EVERY DAY FOR A WHOLE WEEK AND I CAN'T WAIT TO HEAD HOME, TOMORROW!

ED AND MITCH HAVE BEEN NOTHING BUT THE SWEETEST, MOST GRACIOUS AND ACCOMODATING HOSTS.

I'M NOT SAYING THAT THEY HAVEN'T BEEN, LEONARD. BUT GEEZ, I JUST WANT TO GO HOME—I'M NOT AS YOUNG AND ADVENTUROUS AS I USED TO BE. I JUST WANNA GET BACK TO MY OWN BED AND MY OWN BATHROOM. BESIDES, AS "SWEET" AS THEY ARE, ED IS A NEAT FREAK AND MITCH HAS SOME OF THE MOST BIZARRE NOTIONS ABOUT GOURMET COOKING. AND I SIMPLY CANNOT WAIT TO NOT HAVE THEIR TWO, YAPPY, OVER PAMPERED LITTLE DOGS CONSTANTLY UNDERFOOT!

AW, KVETCH, KVETCH, KVETCH!

...OOO! WELL, IT'S NICE TO SEE THAT THE TRIP HASN'T HAD A DETRIMENTAL EFFECT ON YOUR LIBIDO...MMM, I CAN'T REMEMBER THE LAST TIME YOU WERE AMOROUS ENOUGH TO LICK MY EAR.

WHAT?

TRISTAN, ISOLDE! DOWN! GET DOWN OFF THE BED! BAD DOGS, BAD!

...AND THAT'S ANOTHER THING— MITCH AND ED ARE A COUPLE OF RAVING OPERA QUEENS. I HAVE AN EXTREAMLY LOW TOLERANCE FOR PUCCINI TO BEGIN WITH, BUT AFTER AN ENTIRE WEEK AT LA SCALA, WEST...

OH, GIVE IT A REST!

TIM BARELA

45

Panel 1: WELL, I FINALLY GOT LAUREN TO GO TO SLEEP, BUT IT TOOK LETTING HER CUDDLE THAT *HORRID* TEDDY BEAR DRESSED IN *LEATHER* AND *CHAINS* TO DO IT.

THAT'S *WHY* I DON'T MIND BABY-SITTING LAUREN. THE MORE WE GET TO HAVE HER, THE *LESS* OFTEN LAUREN'S *OTHER GRAN'PA* AND HIS "*DOMESTIC PARTNER*" HAVE A CHANCE TO BE SUCH A CONTINUAL *BAD INFLUENCE* ON HER.

Panel 2: I JUST WISH OUR *DEBBIE* WOULD TRY TO BE A *BETTER* INFLUENCE! LETTING A THREE-YEAR-OLD PACK HER OWN OVERNIGHT BAG— *HOW* WILL LAUREN EVER LEARN TO *COORDINATE AND ACCESSORIZE* WITHOUT *PROPER SUPERVISION?!*... AND THEN THERE'S THIS *VIDEO CASSETTE.* LAUREN SAYS THAT IT'S HER "*WEDDING VIDEO*", THAT SHE WAS *THE FLOWER GIRL.* IMAGINE, OUR GRANDDAUGHTER GETTING TO BE THE FLOWER GIRL IN SOMEONE'S WEDDING AND NEITHER DEBBIE NOR RICHARD *EVER* MENTIONING *A WORD* OF IT TO US!

WELL, LET'S STICK IT IN THE OL' VCR AND *HAVE A LOOK.*

Panel 3: THERE'S OUR *PRECIOUS ANGEL!* OH LOOK, PHILIP, ISN'T SHE *ABSOLUTELY ADORABLE?!* OH, HOW COULD DEBBIE *NOT* TELL US OR, AT LEAST, HAVE SHOWN THIS TO US BEFORE NOW?

HUH, I COULD SWEAR THAT I'VE SEEN THAT MAN IN THE COWBOY HAT ON *TV,* BEFORE. AND LOOK, THERE'S SOMEONE ELSE DRESSED LIKE A *MOTORCYCLE COP.* MUST'VE BEEN A REAL *CLASSY GIG!*...BUT *WHY* WOULD A HIRED MOTORCYCLE ESCORT BE AT THE CEREMONY?

LOOK, THOSE PEOPLE WITH BEANIES ON THEIR HEADS, A CANOPY... *WHY,* IT'S A JEWISH WEDDING. I WASN'T AWARE OF OUR DEBBIE KNOWING ANYONE OF THE *JEWISH PERSUASION.*

Panel 4: ...THAT IS, OF COURSE, ANYONE BUT LAUREN'S GRANDFATHER LARRY'S "*FRIEND*", LEONARD. PERHAPS THE HAPPY COUPLE WERE PEOPLE THAT DEBBIE AND RICHARD MET THROUGH LEONARD.

OR— WHO KNOWS— MAYBE IT *WASN'T* SOMEONE ELSE. MAYBE THE HAPPY COUPLE WERE LARRY AND LEONARD!

HA HA HA HA HA HA HA HA

Panel 5: AAGGGHH!!

Panel 6: AT LEAST LAUREN HAD THE BENEFIT OF BEING AROUND PEOPLE WHO— APPARENTLY— DO KNOW HOW TO *COORDINATE* AND *ACCESSORIZE*....AND DO IT SO WELL...

OH GET A GRIP, BARBRA!

THIS IS A NIGHTMARE! WHERE THE HELL IS EVERYBODY?

THIS IS SO COOL! YA KNOW, MOSTA THE TIME, THEY DON'T EVEN LET ME INSIDE THE CLASSICAL ROOM. BUT HERE I AM, DOIN' 'N AUTOGRAPH PARTY WITH A REAL, LIVE, KINDA FAMOUS PIANO GUY, GETTIN' TA DRESS-UP IN ALL THESE BODACIOUS THREADS—JUST LIKE IN "AMADEUS"!... YA KNOW, I SAW PARTS O' THAT MOVIE ONCE. DID YOU EVER SEE THAT MOVIE?

ONCE OR TWICE... YOU PEOPLE HAVE THESE SORTS OF THINGS IN THIS STORE ALL THE TIME—DOESN'T ANYONE EVER SHOW UP?

WELL, THE OTHER SIDE O' THE STORE WAS PACKED FER THAT LAST KURT COBAIN AUTOGRAPH PARTY WE HAD—AND THAT WAS AFTER HE WAS ALREADY DEAD. I GOT TA BE KURT FER THAT ONE 'N' I DIDN'T EVEN NEED A COSTUME!.... WOW, KURT COBAIN 'N' MOZART ARE BOTH DEAD... IT'S KINDA PROFOUND, YA KNOW?

THIS EVENT WAS SUPPOSED TO BE PROMOTED ALONG WITH MY NEW C.D. DIDN'T ANYONE SEND OUT PRESS RELEASES?

WELL SURE.... BUT, LIKE, MAYBE SOMEBODY MADE A MISTAKE... MAYBE SOMEBODY PUT DOWN EIGHT A.M. INSTEAD O' EIGHT P.M.... OR SOMETHIN' LIKE THAT.

DON'T BE RIDICULOUS! UNLESS, OF COURSE, YOU WERE RESPONSIBLE FOR THE PRESS RELEASE. HOW COULD ANYBODY MAKE SUCH AN OBVIOUS AND STUPID MISTAKE? THIS STORE DOESN'T EVEN OPEN TILL TEN!

WELL YEAH... BUT THAT WOULD KINDA EXPLAIN WHY THERE WAS SUCH A BIG CROWD OUT FRONT WHEN I GOT TA WORK THIS MORNING.

MY GAWWWD! I'M SURROUNDED BY FOOLS! I AM BESIEGED AND SURROUNDED BY INCOMPETENTS AND FOOLS AND THEY'RE ALL PLOTTING TOWARDS MY DEMISE.... BIT BY BIT, PIECE OF MY SANITY BY PIECE....

WELL HEY, MAN, YA KNOW THIS GIG WASN'T A TOTAL WASTE. YA STILL HAD THAT ONE OL' WHACKED OUT LADY WHO ASKED FER YER AUTOGRAPH.

...MAN, I REALLY THOUGHT SHE WAS GONNA TOTALLY LOSE IT WHEN YOU GOT UP TA SHAKE HER HAND..."HE CAN WALK, HE CAN WALK—IT'S A MIRACLE!!"... SHE WAS KINDA BUMMED, THOUGH, WHEN SHE FOUND OUT THAT YOU WEREN'T REALLY THAT PEARL GUY.

PERLMAN. SHE THOUGHT I WAS PERLMAN!

...WELL, I'D BE BUMMED, TOO. THAT PEARL MAN GUY IS ONE AWESOME DUDE!

...I STILL CAN'T FIGURE OUT, THOUGH, HOW HE DIVES FER THOSE LI'L OYSTERS WITH HIS CRUTCHES.

YA KNOW, I THINK THAT THE MUSIC YOU NORMALLY LISTEN TO HAS STRAINED YOUR DELICATE BRAIN MUSCLES.

WOW, MAN, YA REALLY THINK SO?

47

Panel 1:

...I'M REAL SORRY THAT I INTERRUPTED YOUR *PARTY*, DAD.

IT'S *NOT* MUCH OF A PARTY; JUST BOB 'N' FRANK 'N' LEONARD 'N' ME HAVING A LITTLE *COOK-OUT*.

WELL, DEBBIE'S FOLKS ARE HERE AND WE'RE GOING OUT TO EAT A LITTLE LATER. **BUT** LAUREN WANTED US TO CALL HER GRAN'PA FIRST. YA SEE, SHE'S STARTED GOING "*POTTY*" ALL BY HERSELF—SHE'S *SO PROUD!* SHE HAD TO HAVE ME GET YOU ON THE PHONE SO SHE COULD TELL HER *GRAN'PA LARRY* ALL ABOUT IT.

OH JOY, A REAL *HALLMARK* MOMENT. LEONARD WILL BE *THRILLED*.

Panel 2:

...SO HANG ON, DAD. LAUREN'S STILL IN THE BATHROOM TAKING CARE OF *DETAILS*, BUT I'LL BE BACK WITH HER IN A MINUTE.

I STILL THINK THAT WE SHOULD SAY SOMETHING ABOUT THE TWO OF US KNOWING ABOUT LAUREN AND GRAND'PA LARRY'S GHASTLY WEDDING VIDEO.

NOT YET! WE HAVE TO APPROACH THIS ISSUE WITH GREAT CARE. AFTER ALL, OUR GRANDDAUGHTER AND HER PROPER UPBRINGING ARE AT STAKE. WE JUST CAN'T RUSH IN AND DO SOMETHING *STUPID*.

Panel 3:

OH, AND TO THINK THAT I HAD ORIGINALLY ASSUMED THAT HAVING A HOMOSEXUAL FOR AN IN-LAW WOULD, SOMEHOW, BE AMUSING.

I WONDER WHAT KIND OF PARTY THEY'RE HAVING...THAT TV PREACHER'S BOOK THAT I'VE BEEN READING CERTAINLY HAS BEEN *ILLUMINATING* AS TO THE DEPRAVITY AND SORDIDNESS OF THE GAY LIFESTYLE—TOPS AND BOTTOMS, CHICKEN HAWKS, WILD S & M SEX ORGIES...THERE'S ONE WAY TO FIND OUT...

Panel 5:

WELL, HERE THEY ARE, HOT OFF THE *RACK*. WHICH WOULD YOU RATHER HAVE, LARRY THE *TOP CHICKEN* OR THE *BOTTOM CHICKEN?*

I DEFINITELY WANT THE *TOP CHICKEN*—THAT BIG, MEATY ONE. UNLESS, OF COURSE, YOU GUYS WOULD RATHER HAVE THE LI'L BUGGER.

OH NO, GO AHEAD 'N' TAKE YER PICK. WE'LL HAVE THE *BOTTOM CHICKEN*, WE'RE NOT FUSSY.

Panel 6:

OH MY GOD!!

WHAT ARE YOU GUYS *DOING?*

I JUST FILLED DAD IN AS TO WHAT'S BEEN GOING ON: HOW YOU GUYS WERE LISTENING IN ON THEIR CONVERSATION WHILE DEBBIE AND I WERE IN THE BATHROOM WITH LAUREN, HOW YOU GUYS THOUGHT THAT THEY WERE HAVING A "WILD S&M SEX ORGY" AND PICKING OUT WHICH CHICKEN TO PORK.

...WELL, THEY'RE ACTUALLY HAVING A COOK-OUT AND THE ONLY CHICKENS INVOLVED USED TO HAVE BEAKS AND FEATHERS; THEY'RE ALL HAVING A GOOD LAUGH RIGHT NOW.

HOW COULD YOU GUYS DO SUCH A THING?!

AND HOW COULD YOU NOT TELL US ABOUT OUR LAUREN BEING THE FLOWER GIRL IN A WEDDING? PARTICULARLY THAT WEDDING!

WE WERE SHOCKED, YOUNG LADY, SHOCKED THAT YOU WOULD ALLOW OUR GRANDDAUGHTER TO BE EXPOSED TO SUCH DEPRAVITY—A WEDDING FOR TWO MEN!

YEAH, TWO MEN WHO LAUREN'S KNOWN ALL HER LIFE AND LOVES, TWO MEN WHO SHE BOTH CALLS GRAN'PA AND ALREADY THINKS OF AS BEING AS MUCH OF A COUPLE AS US OR YOU GUYS.

WE THINK THAT IT WAS A POSITIVE EXPERIENCE FOR HER. MAYBE THAT'S WHY WE DIDN'T TELL YOU. WE KNEW THAT YOUR REACTION WOULD HAVE BEEN NOTHING BUT A NEGATIVE EXPERIENCE.

ALLOWING LAUREN TO SEE HER OTHER GRAN'PA TAKE A STAND FOR TRADITIONAL FAMILY VALUES WOULD NOT BE A "NEGATIVE EXPERIENCE."

AND STUPIDITY IS NOT A TRADITIONAL FAMILY VALUE! BUT TWO PEOPLE PUBLICLY PROFESSING AND COMMITING THEIR LOVE AND LIVES TO ONE ANOTHER IS. AND SO IS LEARNING TO BE OPEN MINDED AND ACCEPTING OF PEOPLE WHO MIGHT BE DIFFERENT THAN YOU ARE.

BUT DEAR, THE MORE YOU EXPOSE LAUREN TO THOSE TYPES OF PEOPLE AND IDEAS, THE LESS SHE MAY WANT TO BE "DIFFERENT." SHE MAY GROW UP WANTING TO BE THE SAME. SHE MIGHT GROW UP TO BE A... A LESBIAN!

OH, GET REAL, MOTHER!

I DIDN'T GROW UP TO BE GAY.

AND I DIDN'T GROW UP TO BE A SNOBBISH, UPTIGHT, EAVESDROPPING HORSE'S REAR END!

OH, WHAT MUST LEONARD AND LARRY AND THEIR FRIENDS BE THINKING?

WILL YOU GUYS PLEASE STOP PLAYING WITH YOUR FOOD?

MY IN-LAWS THINK THAT WE'RE HAVING A "WILD S&M SEX ORGY" WITH THE "BOTTOM CHICKEN" AND I DON'T WANT TO DISAPPOINT THEM.

YEAH, BUT SCALLIONS MAKE LOUSY BULL WHIPS.

JIM BRYGLAS

Panel 1:

...CINDY HARDING, *STAR OF THE HIT COMEDY SERIES, "THE GRASS IS ALWAYS GREENER", IS SEEN HERE AT LAST MONTH'S EMMY PRE-SENTATION ESCORTED BY HER HOT NEW CO-STAR, SUPER HUNK, MERLE OBERON. SERIES HEAD WRITER, BERNIE GOLDMAN FOLLOWS CLOSE BEHIND...*

POOR JIM. THERE'S MERLE, BASKING IN THE GLOW OF HIS SUCCESS AND POOR JIM GETS LEFT OUT IN THE COLD. MERLE USED TO BE SUCH A NICE GUY; HOW COULD HE JUST GO 'N' DUMP JIM LIKE THAT?

Panel 2:

FAME AND MONEY *MAKE PEOPLE ACT STRANGE AND DO* STUPID, SELFISH *THINGS. KINDA LIKE THE OWNER OF JIM'S APARTMENT BUILDING. "RECENTLY DIS-COVERED* EARTHQUAKE DAMAGE" MY ASS! *THAT* GREEDY LITTLE BASTARD *JUST WANTS TO PUT UP A BIGGER BUILDING WITH MORE UNITS, IN IT'S PLACE.*

POOR JIM. *MERLE IN THAT NICE HOUSE UP IN BEVERLY GLEN AND JIM* BANISHED *TO A CON-DEMNED APARTMENT THAT HE HAS TO BE OUT OF BY THE FIRST OF THE YEAR...* WE HAVE TO *DO SOMETHING TO HELP...*

Panel 3:

NO LEONARD! *HAVEN'T YOU HELPED* ENOUGH? *AFTER ALL, YOU'RE THE* MATCHMAKING GENIUS *WHO GOT MERLE AND JIM TOGETHER IN THE FIRST PLACE!*

LARRY, *YOU* OWE IT *TO JIM. WE* NEED *TO HELP HIM IF HE HAS NOWHERE ELSE TO TURN. HE'S BEEN THERE FOR YOU FROM THE BEGINING—YOUR MOST LOYAL EMPLOYEE, SAT WITH YOU FOR THREE DAYS AND NIGHTS HELPING TO* PROTECT *YOUR STORE DURING* THE RIOTS. *ALL I'M TALKING ABOUT IS LETTING JIM* STAY HERE *IF HE NEEDS TO, UNTIL HE FINDS HIS OWN PLACE....AND I* NEVER *WOULD'VE HAD ANYTHING TO PLAY MATCH-MAKER WITH IF* YOUR BROTHER, DALE, *HADN'T* DRAGGED *MERLE* WITH HIM, *OUT HERE FROM TEXAS, TO BEGIN WITH!*

AW GEEZ, *LEONARD!* JIM LIVING HERE, *UNDER THE* SAME ROOF WITH US? *REGARDLESS OF HOW SHORT A TIME THAT MAY BE, ISN'T IT* BAD ENOUGH *THAT I HAVE TO SPEND* EVERY DAY *AT WORK WITH THE MAN? YOU HAVE* NO IDEA *WHAT IT'S BEEN LIKE! ONE DAY HE'S* MOPING *AROUND IN A FUNK, THE NEXT HE'S* STORM-ING *AROUND LOOKING FOR SOMETHING ELSE TO* BREAK— *WHICH,* THANKFULLY, *ISN'T EASY IN A LEATHER SHOP. ...AND JIM WOULDN'T BE HAVING THESE PROBLEMS AND WE WOULDN'T BE HAVING THIS ARGUMENT IF YOUR BROTHER, BERNIE, HADN'T GOTTEN MERLE A PART IN HIS INSIPID SITCOM IN THE LAST PLACE!*

Panel 4:

—SIGH— *LARRY, WHAT WOULD* YOU *DO IN THAT SITUATION? I MEAN, IF YOU SUDDENLY FOUND YOURSELF FAMOUS, LIKE MERLE, WOULD YOU* ABANDON ME *FOR THE GLITZ AND GLAMOR OF THE GOOD LIFE?*

WHAT *DO YOU MEAN "IF" I SUDDENLY FOUND MYSELF "FAMOUS"? I ALREADY* AM. *WHY, PEOPLE EVEN RECOGNIZE ME ON THE STREET.*

THEY DO?

Panel 5:

SURE. *IN FACT, JUST THE OTHER DAY THESE GUYS CAME UP TO ME AND ONE OF THEM SAID,* "HEY, *YOU'RE THE GUY WITH THAT LEATHER SHOP ON MELROSE, THE ONE WHO INVENTED THE 'BUTT PLUG, ONE CENT SALE!'" THEN HE TOLD HIS BUDDY, "THIS MAN'S* REVOLUTIONIZING EROTICA RETAIL; *HE'S* FAMOUS!"

I GUESS I HAVE NOTHING TO WORRY ABOUT.

RIGHT. *I'M MUCH TOO* MATURE *TO LET SOMETHING LIKE THAT GO TO MY HEAD.*

52

Panel 1:

GET REAL, HARRY, THAT'S CHUMP CHANGE! YOU TELL THOSE JOKERS THAT IF THEY WANT ME TA ENDORSE THEIR CRAPPY PRODUCT LINE, THEY'RE GONNA HAVE TA COUGH-UP SOME REAL MONEY!

RESIDUALS? HARRY, I DON'T GIVE A RAT'S ASS ABOUT RESIDUALS WHEN THE INITAL FEE IS THAT PIDDLY. HELL, IF I WANTED TA SELL MYSELF THAT CHEAP I'D PUT ON TIGHT PANTS 'N' GO STAND OUT ON SANTA MONICA BOULEVARD!

Panel 2:

...GIMME A BREAK, HARRY! YA KNOW, THERE'S PLENTY O' OTHER AGENTS IN THIS TOWN WHO'D GIVE THEIR EYE TEETH TA BE HANDLIN' MY CAREER RIGHT ABOUT NOW. IF YOU REALLY WANTED TO, I KNOW THAT YOU COULD —SHIT!!

...NO, NOT YOU, HARRY. I HAD SOME GUY OUT HERE T'DAY INSTALLIN' A NEW DEAD BOLT IN MY FRONT DOOR 'N' THAT IDIOT WENT 'N' PUT A NEW DOOR KNOCKER ON THERE, TOO. YOU SHOULD SEE IT! I MEAN, TALK ABOUT UGLY, THIS THING'S A FUCKIN' GARGOYLE! I SWEAR, IT LOOKS JUST LIKE DEATH CHEWIN' ON A CRACKER.

Panel 3:

DAMN IT, HARRY, DON'T GO PUTTIN' ME ON HOLD!!

I'LL TAKE THAT FOR YOU, DEAR. YOU KNOW, WHEN YOU FINALLY GET AROUND TO DECORATING THIS PLACE, YOU SHOULD CONSIDER ONE OF THOSE ADORABLE BRASS HAT RACKS FOR THE ENTRY. AND, OF COURSE, YOU'LL BE NEEDING CURTAINS. I CAN ENVISION OODLES AND OODLES OF DARLING WHITE LACE... CAN'T YOU?

Panel 4:

...AND WALLPAPER! WALLPAPER ALWAYS ADDS A NICE, COZY TOUCH TO A NEW HOME. WHAT DO YOU THINK OF PALE YELLOW WITH DOZENS AND DOZENS OF TINY, PRECIOUS PINK ROSES?

HUMPH... SO, YOU'RE THE SORRY SPECIMEN THAT WE'LL BE WASTING A PERFECTLY GOOD EVENING WITH. THINK I'M JUST A "FAT, HAIRY OLD MAN", DO YOU? WELL, WE'LL SEE ABOUT THAT.

Panel 5:

HARRY?...YEAH, I'M AFFRAID THAT I'M GONNA HAVE TA CALL YA BACK...WELL, I HAVE TA CALL 911 RIGHT NOW. YA SEE, I JUST GOT HOME AND THERE'S THESE TWO WEIRD BURGLERS IN THE HOUSE....YEAH, WELL, YOU SHOULD SEE 'EM. THEY LOOK LIKE A COUPLE O' REJECTS FROM CENTRAL CASTIN', ALL DRESSED UP IN STUFF THEY GOT AT THE LAST WESTERN COSTUME GARAGE SALE.

Panel 6:

...NAW, I CAN HANDLE IT. I MEAN—SHIT—THE BOTH O' 'EM LOOK TA BE ABOUT A HUNDERD YEARS OLD!

ACTUALLY, THAT WOULD BE 161 AND 154, RESPECTIVELY!

I NEVER ADMIT TO BEING A DAY OVER ONE HUNDRED THIRTY-NINE.

53

SHIT—NEVER FAILS! CALL 911 'N' GET A BUSY SIGNAL!...OK, JUST WHAT ARE YOU GUYS DOIN' HERE?

WELL, IT IS A RATHER STRANGE, ESOTERIC LITTLE RUNNING GAG, BUT A LOT OF THE READERS SEEM TO LIKE IT. YOU SEE, IT ALL HAS TO DO WITH THE CARTOONIST'S LOVE FOR CLASSICAL MUSIC. I'M HIS FAVORITE COMPOSER AND HE'S...WELL, HE'S QUEER.

OH HUSH!

The Grass is always [greener]

WAIT A MINUTE...I RECOGNIZE YOU FELLAS! YOU'RE THOSE DEAD MUSIC GUYS FROM A HUNDERD YEARS AGO, THE FACES IN JIM'S CD BOXES, THE ONES HE SAYS HE TALKS TO IN HIS SLEEP...AND YOU ARE THE QUEER ONE!

WELL, YA KNOW, VICTORIA WASN'T THE ONLY QUEEN WHO HUNG OUT IN THE NINETEENTH CENTURY.

DO YOU MIND?!

I'M NOT REALLY SEEIN' NONE O' THIS! IT'S JUST A BAD DREAM. I NEVER SHOULDA ORDERED THAT LEMON GRASS SOUP IN THE FIRST PLACE—I WILL NEVER EAT THAI FOOD 'N' HAVE BEN 'N' JERRY'S FER DESSERT EVER AGAIN!

I CAN ASSURE YOU, MERLIN DEAR, THAT I AM NOT LEMON GRASS SOUP. WE ARE HERE TO-NIGHT TO HELP YOU MAKE AN ASSESSMENT OF THE HURTFULL, CALLOUS, SELF CENTERED MORASS THAT YOUR LIFE HAS BECOME. YOU SEE, ACCORDING TO THE SCRIPT, WE'RE DOING OUR OWN LITTLE VERSION OF DICKENS' "A CHRISTMAS CAROL". YOU WILL, OBVIOUSLY, BE OUR SCROOGE AND WE, BEING THE ONLY GHOSTS AVAILABLE, WILL FILL IN AS THE SPIRITS OF CHRISTMAS PAST, PRESENT AND FUTURE...

GHOSTS?

Leonard & Larry

...WE'RE GHOSTS?

OF COURSE WE'RE GHOSTS! I'VE BEEN DEAD ONE HUNDRED ONE YEARS, YOU NINETY-SEVEN—WHAT ELSE WOULD WE BE?

HMMM, I'VE NEVER THOUGHT OF US AS BEING GHOSTS. PERHAPS WE SHOULD "FIELD TEST" THIS HYPOTHESIS.

BOO.

ARRGHH!!

OH, I'M GOING TO ENJOY THIS! IN SPITE OF MY BEST EFFORTS, I WAS NEVER ABLE TO SCARE PEOPLE THIS WELL WHEN I WAS ALIVE!

WELL, COME ALONG NOW, MERLIN DEAR. WE HAVE AN APPOINTMENT TO KEEP WITH THE FLEETING SHADOWS OF CHRISTMAS PAST...

ARRGH!

ARRGH!! ...BUT A PERSON CAN'T STAND IN MID-AIR IN FRONT O' A SECOND STORY WINDA! HOW DID I GET INTA MY NIGHT-SHIRT, ANYWAY? IT DOESN'T SNOW IN SANTA MONICA!!

...ABOUT AS LIKELY AS A COUPLE OF DEAD NINETEENTH CENTURY COMPOSERS IN A GAY COMIC STRIP, ISN'T IT?

SPEEK FOR YOURSELF, SWEETIE... NOW, NOW, MERLIN DEAR, ALL OF THIS IS JUST SPECIAL EFFECTS...

...A BIG TV STAR, LIKE YOURSELF, SHOULD KNOW ALL ABOUT THAT SORT OF THING.

...BESIDES, AS I'M SURE YOU REMEMBER, IN THE ORIGINAL STORY SCROOGE WAS IN HIS NIGHTSHIRT WHEN THE SPIRIT TOOK HIM OUT INTO THE SNOW TO STAND BEFORE THE WINDOW AND BEHOLD THE SHADOWS OF CHRISTMAS PAST...

HOLY SH—!!

MY, MY, MY, AREN'T YOU THE TALENTED ONE! TELL ME, DEAR, JUST HOW DID YOU MANAGE TO GET INTO THAT POSITION, ANYWAY? IT REMINDS ME, YOU KNOW, OF A PARTICULARLY ENERGETIC YOUNG MAN WHO I KNEW ONCE... FROM MINSK, I BELIEVE....

TELL ME, PETER, WAS STRAVINSKY'S BALLET, "THE FAIRY'S KISS" REALLY INSPIRED BY YOUR MUSIC... OR YOUR LIFE?

HUSH!

WELL, IT'S NOW A YEAR LATER AND THINGS ARE QUITE A BIT LESS LIVELY SINCE YOU AND OUR DEAR FRIEND JAMES SPENT YOUR FIRST CHRISTMAS TOGETHER.

...OF COURSE, JAMES WASN'T PLEASED TO BE THE NEXT THING SACRIFICED IN FAVOR OF YOUR CAREER AND CONTINUED SUCCESS. BUT THEN, IT IS REMARKABLE HOW BADLY SOME PEOPLE WILL ALLOW THEMSELVES TO BE TREATED WHEN THEY LOVE THE PERPETRATOR.... ISN'T IT?

JIM?

NOW, NOW, REMEMBER THE ORIGINAL STORY; JAMES CAN NEITHER HEAR NOR SEE YOU... THE POOR DEAR, HE JUST HASN'T BEEN HIMSELF SINCE YOU LEFT HIM — THE TORPOR, THE DEPRESSION — HE'S COMPLETELY LOST ALL SELF RESPECT AS THE RESULT OF IT.

...WHY, JUST LOOK AT HIM NOW, ENGAGING IN SOME OF THE MOST VILE, LOATHSOME, SELF DEPRECATING HOLIDAY BEHAVIOR.

AW JIM, I'M SO SORRY! I NEVER THOUGHT THAT I'D HURT YA THIS BAD, THAT I'D DRIVEN YA TA THESE DEPTHS!

HAVE YOU TWENTIETH CENTURY PEOPLE NO SHAME?

HO, HO, HO!

I UNDERSTAND THAT MOUSSORGSKY LIKED CATS; HE HAD A HOUSE FULL OF THEM! BUT THEN, RUSSIANS ARE WEIRD.

I HOPE MERLE'S HAVING A NICE CHRISTMAS, WHEREVER HE IS.

WHATSA MATTER WITH SMOKEY BEAR? WHY'S HE SLEEPIN' IN THAT OLD BOOT BOX?

SHH!

WELL, DEAR, YOU MAY HAVE FORGOTTEN, HAVING MOVED INTO THAT NICE, BIG HOUSE WITHOUT HIM, BUT JAMES' APARTMENT WAS CONDEMNED AND HE HAD TO FIND A NEW HOME BY THE FIRST OF THE YEAR OR BE EVICTED... I'M AFRAID THAT SMOKEY BEAR NEVER DID ADJUST AFTER THE MOVE...

...A YEAR LATER, AROUND CHRISTMAS TIME, HE GOT OUT SOMEHOW, INTO THE STREET AND THE TRAFFIC AND...

NO!

DID YOU REALLY THINK THAT HAPPINESS AND JOY WOULD BE THE END RESULT OF YOUR SELFISHNESS?

WAIT A MINUTE! I REMEMBER HOW THE STORY GOES. SCROOGE IS THE NEXT ONE TA FIND OUT HOW HE DIES. ...I'M NEXT, AREN'T I?

OK, IF YOU INSIST. OF COURSE, DEAR, YOU WON'T BUY THE FARM IN THE USUAL SENSE, YOU'RE GONNA DIE IN THE RATINGS. YOUR AUDIENCE "Q's" WILL BE THE FIRST THING TO HIT THE SKIDS, BUT YOU'LL SOON MANAGE TO DRAG THE REST OF YOUR "HIT" TV SHOW DOWN THE TUBES WITH YOU. IT WILL ALL BE A RESULT OF THE SCANDAL, YOU KNOW, THE STORY ABOUT YOU AND THAT HUNKY, UNDERAGED, YOUNG THING IN THE RESTROOM AT THE '96 EMMY AWARDS PARTY. WITH YOUR FACE SPLASHED ACROSS THE COVERS OF EVERY SUPERMARKET TABLOID ON THE PLANET AND YOUR CAREER IN THE PROVERBIAL LOO, YOU'LL BE FORCED TO APPEAR IN A SERIES OF OBNOXIOUS TV COMMERCIALS, PORTRAYING AN ANTHROPOMORPHISED BOTTLE OF TOILET BOWL CLEANER JUST TO MAKE ENDS MEET.

...AND THOSE NASTY RUST STAINS UNDER THE RIM. YUP, I'VE GOT LOADS O' EXPERIENCE IN BATHROOMS...

ARRGH! NO, THIS CAN'T HAPPEN! PLEEASE! PLEASE TELL ME WHAT I HAVE TA DO TA KEEP THESE THINGS FROM HAPPENIN', WHAT I HAVE TA DO TA PUT THINGS RIGHT AGAIN!!

BUT YOU ALREADY KNOW WHAT TO DO, DEAR. I WISH I COULD TELL YOU THAT IT WAS AS EASY AS CLICKING YOUR HEALS TOGETHER THREE TIMES, BUT IT'S NOT. ADMITTING THAT YOU WERE WRONG IS ALWAYS HARD. FORTUNATELY, THE PERSON THAT YOU HURT SO BADLY STILL LOVES YOU. IF THAT RING ON YOUR FINGER STILL MEANS ANYTHING, YOU'LL BE ABLE TO FIGURE OUT THE REST.

JIM BARELA

ARRGGH!!

IT'S MORNIN', CHRISTMAS MORNIN'. AND I'M BACK, BACK IN MY OWN HOUSE 'N' MY OWN... IT WAS JUST A DREAM—THAT'S ALL—JUST A BIG BAD OL' NASTY NIGHTMARE ...WASN'T IT?

THUMP!
KNOCK
CRASH!

WHO'S OUT THERE? WHAT DO YOU WANT? WHOEVER YOU ARE, BEING THAT IT'S CHRISTMAS MORNING, YOU'D BETTER BE DRESSED LIKE SANTA CLAUS!

MERRY CHRISTMAS! HO, HO, HO!

MERLE! WHAT THE... OH WOW, A GRAY CAT. I'M AFFRAID THAT I ALREADY HAVE ONE OF THOSE... MERLE, WHAT THE HELL ARE YOU DOING HERE? SHOWING UP UNANOUNCED, LURKING AROUND MY APARTMENT AND MY KITCHEN?

IT'S CHRISTMAS! SORRY 'BOUT THE NOISE. I WAS FIXIN' TA MAKE SMOKEY BEAR HIS BREAKFAST, BUT I COULDN'T FIND THE CAT FOOD. WELL, YA KNOW HOW IT IS, MOVING 'N' PACKING, THE HOLIDAYS, LIFE SUCKING 'N' ALL.

AND THAT'S THE REASON WHY I'M HERE. I'VE GOT A BIG SURPRISE FOR YA! JUST GO OVER TA THE WINDA 'N' HAVE A LOOK. MERLE!

A BIG TRUCK.

RIGHT. AND DO YOU HAVE ANY IDEA HOW HARD IT IS TA RENT ONE O' THOSE SUCKERS ON CHRISTMAS DAY? BUT I DID 'N' WE'RE GONNA LOAD IT UP WITH ALL YER FURNITURE 'N' STUFF 'N' GET YOU THE HELL OUT O' THIS DUMP BEFORE THOSE BULLDOZERS COME NEXT WEEK. YER SOFA'S GONNA LOOK MIGHTY FINE IN FRONT O' MY FIREPLACE...

WHAT? SINCE WHEN? I THOUGHT THAT OUR RELATIONSHIP WAS A CAREER LIABILITY FOR A BIG TV STAR LIKE YOU. I THOUGHT YOU WERE BETTER OFF LIVING WITHOUT ME... BESIDES, I'VE ALREADY FOUND ANOTHER PLACE. I GAVE THEM A DEPOSIT...

GET IT BACK. A PERSON CAN ALWAYS GET SOMETHIN' BACK IF THEY WANT IT BAD ENOUGH— CAN'T THEY? I MEAN, ALL YA HAVE TA DO IS SAY, "I'M SORRY, I MADE A STUPID MISTAKE, I WAS WRONG. I THREW AWAY SOMETHIN' THAT WAS PRECIOUS TA ME. I WAS SO FULL O' MYSELF THAT I COULDN'T SEE HOW MUCH I NEEDED IT, HOW MUCH I'D MISS IT, AND NOW I WANT IT BACK."

WHAT IS THIS? SOME KIND OF LAME APOLOGY?! AFTER ALL THE CRAP YOU'VE PULLED, YOU EXPECT ME TO... HOW AM I SUPPOSED TO BELIEVE...?

...YOU'RE GROWING YOUR MUSTACHE BACK.

YEAH, I GUESS SO. MY FANS 'VE BEEN WRITIN'; THEY LIKE ME BETTER WITH IT. O' COURSE, WHAT MY NUMBER ONE FAN THINKS, THAT'S ALL THAT REALLY MATTERS. CINDY 'LL JUST HAVE TA SUFFER THRU ALL THOSE KISSIN' SCENES.

OH, THAT SOUNDS WONDERFUL! ...I'VE MISSED YOU, TOO. YA KNOW, WE CAN JUST MOVE THE BIG STUFF TODAY. THAT WOULD LEAVE US ENOUGH TIME TO MAKE A NICE CHRISTMAS DINNER AND MAKE, YA KNOW, OTHER STUFF...

...WE COULD CUDDLE ON THE SOFA AND WE COULD LIGHT A FIRE....IN THE FIREPLACE AND WE COULD LISTEN TO CHRISTMAS MUSIC...

YEAH!

SURE.

...IN FACT, I JUST GOT A NEW RECORDING OF "THE NUTCRACKER SUITE." YA KNOW, THE BALLET BY TCHAIKOVSKY.

ANYTHING YA WANT, HON... BY THE WAY, THE LITTLE FAT ONE WITH THE CIGAR, HE DIDN'T WRITE CHRISTMAS MUSIC TOO, DID HE?

YA MEAN, BRAHMS? WELL, NOTHING LIKE THIS. BESIDES, I DON'T HAV—

GOOD!

..."LITTLE FAT ONE WITH THE CIGAR"?

58

OH GREAT—JURY DUTY! ...DAMN, AND THEY WANT ME THE WEEK THAT I HAVE TO BE IN MAUI DOING THE PHOTOS FOR THAT BIG LAYOUT! THE AGENCY'S ALREADY MADE TRAVEL AND HOTEL RESERVATIONS FOR ME AND EVERYTHING!

AND, IN THE MEANTIME, I GET TO STAY HOME EATING LEFTOVERS AND KEEPING THE HOME FIRES BURNING WHILE YOU SNAP PICTURES OF SKINNY, SCANTILY CLAD, OVER PAID MODELS FROLICKING IN THE SURF IN PARADISE —LIFE'S TOUGH, AIN'T IT?

LARRY, THAT JOB IS GOOD FOR SEVERAL HOUSE PAYMENTS, THE PROPERTY TAX BILL AND THEN SOME! WE CANNOT AFFORD MY CANCELING OUT FOR JURY DUTY.

WELL, THEN FILL OUT THE FORM AND INCLUDE A LETTER—A REAL TEAR JERKER ABOUT THE HARD-SHIPS OF BEING SELF-EMPLOYED, OF HAVING TO WORK YOUR SHUTTER BUTTON FINGER TO THE BONE UNDER THE HOT HAWAIIAN SUN.

THE LAST TIME YOU PULLED JURY DUTY, YOU WERE ONLY THERE FOR ONE DAY...

...YOU NEVER TOLD ME WHAT HAPPENED. HOW DID YOU MANAGE TO GET OUT OF IT?

AH YES, THAT WAS MY FINEST HOUR...

...WE ARE CONCERNED THAT POTENTIAL IM-PROPRIETIES OR CONFLICTS OF INTEREST MAY ARISE WITH YOU AS PROSPECTIVE JURORS. SO, LADIES AND GENTLEMAN, THE FIRST THING I NEED TO KNOW IS IF ANY OF YOU MAY BE RELATIVES OR FRIENDS OF ANYONE WITH THE LAPD, THE CHP OR ANY OTHER LOCAL POLICE AGENCY, THE DISTRICT ATTORNEY'S OFFICE OR ANY EMPLOYEE HERE AT THE LOS ANGELES COUNTY COURTHOUSE...

YES, IN THE FIRST ROW. UMMM... MR. EVANS.

WELL, YOUR HONOR, NONE OF THE ABOVE. HOWEVER, I DO BELIEVE THAT YOU MAY BE ONE OF MY REGULAR CUSTOMERS.

THAT IS, AT MY LEATHER SHOP UP ON MELROSE...

MR. EVANS, YOU ARE HEREBY EX-CUSED FROM THIS COURTROOM AND ANY FURTHER JURY SERVICE OBLIGATIONS. BAILIFF, PLEASE ESCORT MR. EVANS OUT OF THE BUILDING.

...NOW I REMEMBER. YOU CAME IN RECENTLY AND PURCHASED THAT STUDDED LEATHER BODY HARNESS THAT YOU SAID YOU WANTED TO WEAR UNDER YOUR ROB—

MOVE YER BUTT, BAILIFF!

SOUNDS TO ME LIKE YOU JUST MANAGED TO LOSE YOURSELF A GOOD CUSTOMER.

YEAH, BUT IT WAS REALLY WORTH IT.

TIM BARELA

LARRY'S DAY IN COURT, EPISODE II...

BAILIFF, I TRUST THAT YOU ESCORTED THAT TROUBLE MAKING PROSPECTIVE JUROR OUT OF THE BUILDING AND SAW HIM ON HIS WAY AS PER MY INSTRUCTIONS.

YES SIR.

GOOD. INCIDENTLY, I CALLED A RECESS IN YOUR ABSENCE AND HAVE ALREADY SPOKEN WITH THE COURT REPORTER AND BOTH ATTORNEYS. AS FAR AS YOU SHOULD BE CONCERNED, BAILIFF... WELL, IF I WERE YOU, I WOULD THINK IT BEST TO SIMPLY FORGET ABOUT ALL THAT NONSENSE THAT WAS SAID THIS MORNING.

BEGGING YOUR HONOR'S PARDON, BUT MR. EVANS DID EXPRESSLY STATE THAT HE KNOWS YOU, THAT YOU'RE ONE OF HIS CUSTOMERS... YOUR HONOR ISN'T REALLY WEARING ONE OF THOSE LEATHER BODY THINGS... UNDER YOUR... RIGHT NOW ARE YOU?

OFFICER RAMIREZ, ANY NUMBER OF OTHERWISE "NORMAL" PEOPLE IN THIS CITY, AT ANY GIVEN TIME, MAY BE WEARING ALL SORTS OF BIZARRE, KINKY THINGS UNDER THEIR CLOTHING. WHY, YOU, YOURSELF, MAY BE WEARING BOXER SHORTS, TODAY, EMBLAZONED WITH TINY PINK HEARTS—HERE, IN MY CHAMBERS AND IN MY COURTROOM—AND THAT STILL DOESN'T MAKE IT ANY OF MY BUSINESS!

UH, BEGGING YOUR HONOR'S PARDON, BUT I NEVER WEAR BOXER SHORTS. I TEND TO WEAR BIKINI BRIEFS... TODAY THEY'RE RED, SIR.

I'M SURE THAT THEY'RE LOVELY, BAILIFF.

AND I HAVE NO DOUBT THAT YOUR HONOR WOULD INDEED THINK SO.

... I JUST HAVE ONE OTHER QUESTION, SIR. GRANTED, AN INDIVIDUAL'S CHOICE OF "UNDERGARMENTS" AND/OR HARDWEAR AND ACCESSORIES MAY BE A PERSONAL MATTER. HOWEVER, EVEN THE MOST ARDENT ENTHUSIAST FAILS TO WEAR THE SAME THING EVERY DAY. AND YET, YOU'VE SET OFF THE STAFF ENTRANCE METAL DETECTOR SO OFTEN, WE ROUTINELY JUST WAVE YOU AROUND, ANY MORE...

... ALL THOSE LITTLE "HOT SPOTS" ON YOUR BODY, THOSE REALLY AREN'T "SHRAPNEL FROM VIETNAM", ARE THEY?

NO, BAILIFF. BUT YOU HAVE NO IDEA HOW MUCH I WOULD RATHER BE BACK THERE, RIGHT NOW, TAKING A LAND MINE IN MY REAR END, THAN HAVING THIS CONVERSATION WITH YOU!

OOO, SOUNDS PAINFUL, SIR. OF COURSE, I TAKE IT, THAT IS WHAT MAKES IT EXCITING. ... DOESN'T IT?

... AND NOW BACK TO OUR REGULARLY SCHEDULED CAST OF CHARACTERS

60

WHY, YOU'RE BEETHOVEN! WHAT ARE YOU DOING HERE? WHAT'S GOING ON? WHAT'S HAPPENING TO ME?
MY SOURCES INFORM ME THAT, AT THE MOMENT, YOU'RE GOING THRU AN EXTREMELY TRAUMATIC, LIFE THREATENING EXPERI-ENCE AND, AS THE RESULT, YOUR MIND HAS RETREATED INTO A STATE OF FANTASY, THE REASON FOR MY APPEARENCE.
OF COURSE, JUST ABOUT EVERY OTHER DEAD COMPOSER OF NOTE HAS BEEN A GUEST STAR OR THE BUTT OF JOKES IN THIS COMIC STRIP. I SUPPOSE IT WAS JUST MY TURN... IT MUST HAVE SOMETHING TO DO WITH THAT NEW MOVIE ABOUT ME.
...GARY OLDMAN! OF ALL PEOPLE TO PLAY ME, GARY OLDMAN? I WAS, PERSONALLY, HOLDING OUT FOR TOM CRUISE, BUT WHO CARES WHAT I THINK!
BY THE WAY, JUST WHAT KIND OF A "TRAUMATIC, LIFE THREATENING EXPERIENCE" AM I GOING THRU, ANYWAY ?
YOU'RE BEING HELD HOSTAGE AT GUN POINT IN A PARTICULARLY EMBARRASSING STATE OF UNDRESS BY SOME SQUASHED BLOSSOM OF WOMANKIND WHO SEEMS TO BE OBSESSED WITH YOU AND THE MUSIC OF MOZART... NOT AT ALL SURPRISING, REALLY; OL' WOLFBREATH WAS A TOTAL LOON, HIMSELF.
OH YEAH, NOW I REMEMBER. GEEZ, THAT LADY'S A REAL NUT CASE! SHE ESCAPES FROM JAIL AND TAKES THE BUS STRAIGHT DOWN HERE JUST TO MAKE ME PLAY MOZART FOR HER! SHE GOT TIRED OF IT AFTER A WHILE, THOUGH. SHE ASKED TO HEAR "FLUR D'LEASE" FOR A CHANGE OF PACE. THAT'S WHY I WAS THINKING ABOUT YOU, I GUESS.
JIM BARELA
...BY THE WAY, HOW AM I DOING? PLAYING YOUR MUSIC, THAT IS.
I CAN SAY THAT, ABSOLUTELY AND WITHOUT HESITATION, YOUR PLAYING MAKES ME WISH THAT I WERE ALIVE AGAIN.
REALLY?! AND WHY DO YOU SAY THAT ?
BECAUSE, AT THE TIME I WAS...
...DEAF!! I SAID, ARE YOU DEAF?! THAT'S NOT FLUR D' LEASE! JUST WHAT IS THAT CRAP YOU'RE PLAYING?
ARRGGH!!
OH, NEVER MIND. JUST PLAY EINER KLI-NER NOCK MUSIC AGAIN AND MOVE YOUR PRETTY LITTLE BUTT!

HEY, I THOUGHT THAT I WAS GETTING SOME HASH BROWNS, TOO.

OOPS, CHEF'S MISTAKE. WE'LL JUST SEND IT BACK TO THE KITCHEN 'N' FIX IT FOR YA IN NO TIME, HON. SO JUST SIT TIGHT 'N' KEEP YER CLOTHES ON.

HA, HA, VERY FUNNY.

I WANT TO THANK YOU GUYS, AGAIN, FOR LETTING US SLEEP HERE. AFTER WHAT HAPPENED LAST NIGHT, BOB WAS JUST WAY TOO UPSET TO STAY AT OUR PLACE.

INDEED. THERE IS SIMPLY NOTHING MORE UNSETTLING FOR ANY PERFORMING ARTIST THAN TO COME HOME AND FIND A CRAZED CELEBRITY STALKER WITH A GUN LEAPING OUT OF THE BUSHES. ...WELL, PERHAPS IT WOULD BE EVEN MORE UNSETTLING TO COME HOME AND FIND NEWT PIGLET LEAPING OUT OF THE BUSHES WITH HIS BUDGET CUTTING AX, BUT THAT'S ANOTHER NIGHTMARE.

SO HOW DID THE POLICE FIND OUT WHAT WAS GOING ON?

SHE MADE BOB HANDCUFF ME TO THE COAT RACK IN THE HALL CLOSET— WITH MY HANDCUFFS! OF COURSE, SHE DIDN'T KNOW THAT ONE OF THE BUTTONS FOR OUR SILENT ALARM WAS IN THERE WITH ME.

AND THE POLICE WOULD HAVE GOTTEN THERE EVEN SOONER IF BRUNO THE WONDER DOG HADN'T FINALLY DECIDED TO SHOW UP AND HOLD THEM AT BAY ON THE FRONT LAWN!

...EVENTUALLY THEY MADE IT INSIDE AND CORNERED LITTLE MISS SUNSHINE AT THE OTHER END OF THE LIVING ROOM. THEN SHE PUT THAT FUNNY LITTLE GUN IN HER MOUTH AND STARTED PULLING THE TRIGGER AND I THOUGHT, OH GAWWD AND WE JUST HAD THE CARPET CLEANED!

...THE DAMN THING WAS NOTHING BUT A FUCKING CANDY DISPENSER! I WAS STRIPPED AND HUMILIATED AND HELD HOSTAGE BY SOME FRUITCAKE WIELDING A LATTER DAY, RAMBOIZED RIPOFF OF PEZ!!

AND ME, HANDCUFFED TO THE COAT RACK IN THE HALL CLOSET AND NOT ABLE TO WATCH ANY OF THIS!

I SWEAR, THIS WILL NOT HAPPEN AGAIN! THIS TIME, I'M GONNA MAKE SURE THAT THEY LOCK-UP THAT NUTCASE AND THROW THE KEY AWAY! THIS TIME, WHEN I GO TA COURT, I'M GONNA SEE TO IT, I'M GONNA HAVE A CHOICE THING 'R TWO TA TELL THAT JUDGE!

...AND SO, THE DEFENDANT HELD YOU HOSTAGE AT GUN POINT WITH A MINIATURE ASSAULT WEAPON SHAPED CANDY DISPENSER, FORCED YOU TO STRIP NAKED AND PLAY MOZART, SHACKLED TO THE PEDALS OF YOUR PIANO WITH LEATHER BONDAGE GEAR THAT WAS ALREADY KEPT THERE IN YOUR HOME.... I'M AFRAID, MR. MENDEZ, THAT I'M GOING TO REQUIRE MUCH MORE DETAILED TESTIMONY ON YOUR PART BEFORE I CAN RENDER MY DECISION.... MUCH, MUCH MORE...

TIM BARELA

Panel 1:

LARRY, I SWEAR, THOSE LEATHER PANTS ARE GETTING **SO TIGHT** THEY COULD **LOSE** THEIR PG RATING.

AW, **LIGHTEN UP, LEONARD!** SO I GAINED A FEW POUNDS SINCE I LAST WORE THESE. ALL AND ALL, IT JUST HELPS TO **ACCENTUATE MY ATTRIBUTES.**

...SO, WHA'D'YA **THINK?** THIS OUTFIT **NEEDS** SOMETHING ACCESSORY WISE, BUT WHAT? HOW ABOUT **WHIPS?**

WELL, YOU HAVE PLENTY OF CHAINS.

OH, DON'T BE **SILLY, LEONARD.** ...I ALREADY HAVE A **LITTLE** ONE HANGING FROM MY BELT.

Panel 2:

WHY DO WE HAVE TO GO THROUGH THIS EVERY **TIME** WE DRIVE UP HERE TO SPEND A FEW DAYS?

"GO THROUGH" WHAT?

THIS **LEATHER RITUAL,** THAT'S WHAT. WHENEVER WE COME TO SAN FRANCISCO YOU HAVE TO PACK JUST ABOUT **EVERY** PIECE OF **DEAD COW** THAT YOU OWN AND THEN TRY TO WEAR IT **ALL AT ONCE.**

IT'S LIKE THE **MOUNTAIN,** DEAR—BECAUSE **IT'S THERE.** OR, RATHER, BECAUSE **I CAN.** I MEAN, **WHERE ELSE** COULD I DRESS LIKE THIS IN THE MIDDLE OF THE WEEK, IN THE MIDDLE OF THE DAY, AND GET AWAY WITH IT? CERTAINLY NOT BACK HOME. NOT EVEN ON **SANTA MONICA BOULEVARD.**

Panel 3:

...BUT THIS IS SAN FRANCISCO. THIS IS THE CITY WHERE A MAN LIKE ME CAN WALK DOWN **CASTRO STREET** WITH HIS CHEST OUT AND HIS HEAD HELD HIGH AND **SHOUT** TO THE WORLD, "I'M HERE, I'M QUEER, I'M KINKY AND I'M PROUD!"

YEAH, BUT TODAY WE'RE GONNA RIDE THE HYDE STREET **CABLE CAR** OVER THE HILL TO FISHERMAN'S WARF AND SHOP FOR **SOUVENIRS** FOR YOUR **GRANDDAUGHTER.**

YEAH. AND I JUST **LOVE** TO WATCH THE **TOURISTS** FROM NEBRASKA SQUIRM WHEN I SQUEEZE IN BETWEEN THEM AND GIVE 'EM **ATTITUDE!**

64

65

YOO-HOO, JAMES DEAR... COME ALONG NOW, YOU HAVE VISITORS...

PETE!

HELLO DEAR. JUST THOUGHT WE'D POP IN AND SEE HOW THINGS WERE FOR YOU AND MERLIN THESE DAYS.

OH, JUST WONDERFUL! EVERYTHING'S BACK TO NORMAL.

HOW SWEET! BY THE WAY, I ABSOLUTELY LOVE WHAT YOU'VE DONE WITH THE HOUSE! YOU KNOW, ONE OF MY OLD MUSIC STUDENTS USED TO HAVE A LITTLE PLACE NOT FAR FROM HERE...

...SERGEI RACHMANINOFF. MADE GOOD AND DID HIS OL' TEACHER PROUD, JUST LIKE YOU.

AW, THANKS PETE....WE REALLY NEED MORE FURNITURE, THOUGH. MERLE HAS A WHOLE BUNCH IN STORAGE BACK IN TEXAS...

MERLE IS DOING THE FINAL EPISODE OF HIS TV SHOW FOR THE SEASON. NEXT MONTH HE HAS TO BE IN NEW ORLEANS FOR A MINI-SERIES. WE PLAN TO DRIVE THE TRUCK OUT AS FAR AS TYLERVILLE, I GET TO DRIVE BACK WITH THE FURNITURE AND MERLE CONTINUES ON TO RE-FIGHT THE CIVIL WAR... I'M REALLY KIND'VE NERVOUS ABOUT MEETING MERLE'S PARENTS AND SISTER.

OH, NONSENSE! MERLIN IS SIMPLY PROUD OF YOU AS WELL; WANTS TO SHOW YOU OFF. BESIDES, WE HAVE TO PUT UP WITH THESE LITTLE THINGS IN ORDER TO KEEP OUR MEN HAPPY.

THAT'S RIGHT.

AND WHAT WOULD YOU KNOW ABOUT KEEPING A MAN HAPPY?

WELL, I KNOW WHAT NOT TO DO... REMEMBER MY OLD FRIEND JOSEPH, THE VIOLINIST?

YOU MEAN THAT HUNKY HUNGARIAN? THE SEXY ONE WITH THE RAVEN HAIR AND SMOLDERING EYES?

IF YOU SAY SO... ANYWAY, JOSEPH WAS BI OR, AT LEAST, VERY, VERY CONFUSED.

...AND SUCH A TOUCHY, FEELY TYPE; NEVER COULD KEEP HIS HANDS OFF OF ME! WHEN ON TOUR TOGETHER, WE OFTEN HAD TO SHARE A ROOM AND A BED. I PRACTICALLY HAD TO FIGHT HIM OFF MOST OF THE TIME! IT WASN'T UNUSUAL, IN THE DEAD OF NIGHT, TO HEAR HIM WHIMPERING, "DEAR JOHANNES, COME OVER HERE AND SHOW US SOME LOVE." I ALWAYS KEPT MY BACK TURNED TO HIM AND PRETENDED TO BE ASLEEP, OF COURSE. THE POOR, DE-LUDED MAN ALWAYS SOBBED HIMSELF TO SLEEP.

WHY, YOU HEARTLESS, INSENSITIVE, SELFISH BRUTE! WHY...WHY... WHY COULDN'T I HAVE HAD HORNY HUNGARIANS THROWING THEMSELVES AT MY BACKSIDE?!!

SOME OF US GOT IT 'N' SOME OF US AIN'T.

YUP. EVERYTHING'S BACK TO NORMAL.

TIM BARELA

66

WAKE UP, SLEEPYHEAD! WE'VE GOTTA LOOK FER A PLACE TA HAVE BREAKFAST AND THEN YOU GET TA TAKE OVER.

AW, JUST LET ME DOZE A LITTLE LONGER. I'M SAVING MY ENERGY FOR THE EXCITEMENT OF DRIVING THRU TRUTH OR CONSIQUENCES.

OPEN YER EYES 'N' CHECK IT OUT, TOTO, I DON'T THINK WE'RE IN NEW MEXICO ANY MORE.

IS THAT TEXAS?

THE ONE 'N' ONLY, MY OLD HOME, THE LONE STAR STATE, MILES 'N' MILES O' MILES 'N' MILES.

IT KINDA LOOKS LIKE THE SAN JOAQUIN VALLEY WITH A GLAND CONDITION.

WE SHOULD BE IN TYLERVILLE BY SUPPER TIME.

WOW! LOOK AT ALL THE LUPINE GROWING ALONG SIDE THE HIGHWAY; ACRES AND ACRES OF IT! I'VE NEVER SEEN THIS MUCH LUPINE IN BLOOM BEFORE—NOT IN CALIFORNIA.

NOW JIM, REMEMBER, THEY CALL 'EM BLUE BONNETS HERE. THEY'RE THE STATE FLOWER. FOLKS IN THESE PARTS 'R' REAL TOUCHY 'BOUT THAT SORT O' THING. YA HAVE TA BE REAL CAREFUL 'BOUT HOW YA SAY 'N' DO STUFF; THEY DON'T WARM UP TA FOREIGNERS ALL THAT EASY.

GEEZ, YA MAKE IT SOUND LIKE WE JUST CROSSED THE BORDER OF A HOSTILE, THIRD 'N' A HALF WORLD COUNTRY! LIKE THEY'RE GONNA COME AFTER ME 'N' MAKE ME EAT GRITTS AT GUNPOINT 'N' LISTEN TA OLD WILLIE NELSON RECORDS WHEN THEY FIND OUT THAT I DON'T HAVE A VISA!

...MERLE, I JUST KNOW THAT I'M GONNA SCREW-UP. I MEAN, NOT SO MUCH WITH THE GENERAL POPULACE, IT'S YOUR FAMILY I'M REALLY WORRIED ABOUT. THIS IS THE FIRST TIME THAT A GUY'S EVER TAKEN ME HOME TO MEET HIS FOLKS!

AW JIM, WILL YOU STOP WORRYIN'!

...YOU'RE GONNA DO JUST FINE. MY FAMILY ALREADY KNOWS ABOUT US AND THEY KNOW GOOD 'N' WELL THAT IF I'M GONNA COME BACK 'N' VISIT THEY HAFTA TREAT YOU EVER' BIT AS GOOD AS THEY TREAT ME. BESIDES, I'VE BEEN AWAY FER NEARLY THREE YEARS! I'M COMIN' BACK FROM L.A. SUCCESSFUL 'N' FAMOUS, THE MAN THAT I LOVE STANDIN' BY MY SIDE. MY FOLKS 'R' GONNA WELCOME US WITH OPEN ARMS!

JIM BARELA

MOMMA, DADDY, I'M HOME!

OUR SON, THE HOLLYWOOD PERVERT, IS HERE.

I WILL ALERT THE TABLOID PRESS.

WELL, THE BARBECUE'S NEARLY DONE. WE KIN START EATIN' PURDY SOON. THERE'S PLENTY O' POTATO SALAD 'N' BEANS 'N' CORN-ON-THE-COB... AW C'MON EVER'BODY, THIS IS SUPPOSED TA BE A PARTY! IT ISN'T EVER' DAY THAT MY LITTLE BROTHER, THE BIG TV STAR, COMES HOME TA VISIT!

AND I REALLY APPRECIATE YA GOIN' TA ALL THIS TROUBLE FER ME, MAVIS, BUT MAYBE YA SHOULDA JUST USED PROZAC INSTEAD O' SUGAR WHEN YA FIXED THE ICED TEA.

AW, EVER'BODY'S JUST AS EXCITED TA SEE YA AS I AM —AREN'T Y'ALL?—THEY'RE JUST KEEPIN' IT TA THEMSELVES. OH, MOMMA WAS KINDA UPSET YESTERDAY, SOME NONSENSE ABOUT MERLE'S "LIFESTYLE" 'N' NOT "MAKIN' GRANDBABIES" TA "CARRY ON THE FAMILY NAME." I TOLD HER TA STOP BEIN' SILLY. AFTER ALL, WE HAVE MY BOY, ARLO, TA DO THAT!

AREN'T WE LUCKY THAT YA WEREN'T MARRIED AT THE TIME.

BY THE WAY, MAVIS, WHY HAS YER FIANCÉ BEEN STANDIN' OFF BY HIMSELF UNDER THIS CHINA BERRY TREE ALL EVENIN', LOOKIN' LIKE A SCARED CHIHUAHUA?

MAYBE IT'S 'CAUSE HE'S A PINHEAD.

ARLO!... OH, IT'S PROB'LY 'CAUSE WENDEL, HERE, IS SUCH A BIG FAN O' YER TV SHOW. HE WAS JUST THRILLED ABOUT MEETIN' YA! AND WHEN HE FOUND OUT THAT HE'D ALSO BE MEETIN' YER LOVER 'N' ALL, WELL, BEIN' A DEACON AT THE TYLERVILLE FIRST BAPTIST CHURCH, WENDEL WAS THRILLED SPEECHLESS.

...NOW, I TOLD WENDEL THAT, IF HE REALLY WANTS ME TA BE MRS. DUBBS SOMEDAY SOON, HE'S GONNA HAFTA ACCEPT MY BROTHER FER WHO HE IS. IN FACT, I TOLD WENDEL THAT, IF HE REALLY LOVES ME, HE'D SAY AT LEAST ONE NICE THING TA MERLE 'N' JIM, T'NIGHT. MY SWEETIE'S BEEN PRACTICIN' ALL DAY. ...GO ON, WENDIE...SHOW 'EM.

MY GAWWD, THEY'VE BOTH GOT LONG HAIR!!

NOW, YA SEE, THAT WASN'T SO HARD, WAS IT?

I'M IRISH CATHOLIC, TOO. I USED TO DATE A PRIEST BEFORE I MET YOUR FUTURE BROTHER-IN-LAW.

SWEET GEEZ-US IN HEAVEN ABOVE!

DON'T MIND ME, NONE. I'M JUST COMIN' IN HERE TA LISTEN TA MY RADIO.

WELL, OF COURSE NOT, MRS. OBERON. AFTER ALL, THIS IS YOUR KITCHEN... MRS. OBERON, I'VE BEEN MEANING TO THANK YOU FOR YOUR HOSPITALITY, PLAYING HOST TO US. I KNOW THAT ALL THIS HASN'T BEEN EASY FOR YOU...

...I MEAN, ALL THIS STUFF ABOUT ME 'N' MERLE.

BOOM!

"HASN'T BEEN EASY"? MISTER, THIS WHOLE BUSINESS'S BEEN ONE BIG, UGLY ARMADILLA DIGGIN' UP MY PEA PATCH! HELL, FER YEARS I'VE BEEN LOOKIN' FORWARD TA MY MERLE FINALLY SETTLIN' DOWN. WHEN HE DID, THOUGH, I DIDN'T EXACTLY THINK THAT YOU'D BE WHAT HE'D BE BRINGIN' HOME TA MEET MOMMA!

RUMBLE RUMBLE RUMBLE

...I MEAN, JUST LOOK AT YA; YER ANOTHER MAN! AND YER SO BIG 'N' HAIRY!

YER NOT WHAT I HAD IN MIND, WHAT I'D BEEN HOPIN' FOR 'N' LOOKIN' FORWARD TO ALL THESE YEARS... YA SEE, WHEN MY MERLE WAS JUST A BOY HE ALWAYS USED TA SAY TA ME, "WHEN I GROW UP 'N' GET MARRIED, I'M GONNA FIND ME A PRETTY LADY JUST LIKE MY MOMMA".

...WELL, THAT'S NOT EXACTLY HOW THINGS TURNED OUT, IS IT? THERE'S NOTHIN' I KIN DO 'R SAY, SO, IF YA DON'T MIND, I'M JUST GONNA SIT HERE WITH MY RADIO 'N' TAKE A PAUSE FROM MY TROUBLES BY LISTENIN' TA SOMEONE ELSE'S TRAGEDY... THEY'RE DOIN' A LIVE MET BROADCAST T'NIGHT— "LA TRAVIATA". I JUST LOVE "LA TRAVIATA".

REALLY? CAN I STAY AND LISTEN, TOO? THAT'S ONE OF MY FAVORITE OPERAS!

IT IS?

JIM BARELA

OH YEAH! I ESPECIALLY LOVE THE THIRD ACT, DON'T YOU? YA KNOW, THE PART WHERE VIOLETTA IS SO SICK AND ALFREDO RETURNS TO HER AND ALL IS FORGIVEN? I ALWAYS CRY AT THE END WHEN SHE DIES IN HIS ARMS.

OH, SO DO I! EVER' TIME I HEAR THAT PART, I GET JUST LIKE THE BRAZOS RIVER AT FLOOD TIME!

THIS IS SCARY.

OF COURSE, YOU'LL WANT TO LISTEN WITH A STEAMING CUP OF CHAMOMILE TEA.

YES, BUT NO SUGAR. I TAKE HONEY.

YES! I KNOW!

69

Panel 1:

...AFTER I DROPPED MERLE OFF AT THE AIRPORT, ON THE WAY BACK BETWEEN FORT WORTH AND TYLERVILLE, I DROVE THRU THIS **HELLACIOUS** THUNDER STORM —LIGHTNING 'N' RAIN 'N' HAIL LIKE YOU **WOULDN'T BELIEVE!** THEN, ALL OF A SUDDEN, I DROVE OUT OF THE RAIN AND SAW THIS **TORNADO** OFF IN THE DISTANCE, KICKING UP DUST AND GLOWING **RED** IN SUNSET. TALK ABOUT **FREAKY!** I FELT LIKE I COULD'VE BEEN **SUCKED-UP** AND CARRIED OFF TO **THE LAND OF OZ!**

BIG DEAL. OZ WOULD'VE BEEN A **REAL BORE** FOR ANYONE WHO'S BEEN TO **TEXAS** AND **LIVES IN THE LAND OF LA.**

NIC! ELROSE

LARRY'S LEATHER

Panel 2:

MERLE'S MOM IS **GREAT;** WE'RE **BEST PALS** NOW. SHE TAUGHT ME HOW TO MAKE REAL TEXAS STYLE BISCUITS 'N' GRAVY AND GAVE ME A WHOLE BOX OF THESE **PEANUT PATTY** THINGS TO TAKE HOME. MERLE LOVES 'EM AND YOU **CAN'T** FIND THEM ANYWHERE ELSE.

THE **GASTRON-OMIC PROWESS** OF A CULTURE THAT WOULD CONCEIVE OF SUCH THINGS FAIRLY **BOGGLES THE MIND.**

...AND WHEN I GOT HOME I FOUND **THIS** IN THE MAIL...

Panel 3:

...IT'S A PHOTO OF MERLE IN **COSTUME** STANDING IN FRONT OF THAT BIG HOUSE NEAR NEW ORLEANS WHERE THEY'RE SHOOTING SOME OF THE EXTERIORS FOR HIS **MINI SERIES.** DOESN'T MY SWEETIE LOOK **HOT** IN HIS **CONFEDERATE UNIFORM?** THANK YOU, KEN BURNS!

LOOKS TO ME MORE LIKE, **THANK YOU LOUISIANA HUMIDITY...** I RECEIVED A PHOTO MYSELF, LATELY. SORT OF A **FORTY-THIRD** BIRTH-DAY PRESENT.

PEANUT PATTY 69¢

Panel 4:

WHAT THE HELL IS **THIS? CASPER THE FRIENDLY GHOST?** OR MAYBE **HOWARD THE DUCK?**

THAT IS THE FIRST "OFFICIAL" PHOTOGRAPH OF MY NEW **GRANDSON, ENUTERO.** YUP, IT WON'T BE LONG NOW; SOON THERE WILL BE **TWO.** AND—GET THIS— THEY WANT **ME** TO DEFINITELY BE THERE **THIS** TIME, WHEN THE BLESSED EVENT HAPPENS! THEY HAVE **LAMAZE** CLASSES ALL LINED UP FOR ME TO ATTEND WITH **DEBBIE,** MY DAUGHTER-IN-LAW.

Panel 5:

BUT WHY YOU?

SPORTSWEAR. THAT SURFBOARD MANUFACTURER THAT MY SON, **RICHARD,** WORKS FOR HAS A NEW LINE OF SPORTSWEAR. THEY'RE INTRODUCING IT AT A TRADE SHOW AT SOME BIG SURFING COMPETITION IN **HAWAII** JUST BEFORE THE BABY'S DUE. **BIG** OPPORTUNITY FOR RICHARD, CAREER WISE. **BIG** OPPORTUNITY FOR **ME,** GRAN'PA WISE, JUST IN CASE THIS ONE DECIDES TO **POP OUT EARLY** LIKE HIS SISTER BEFORE HIM.

AND, OF COURSE, YOU **STOOD YOUR GROUND LIKE A MAN** AND TOLD THEM "**NO!**"

YOU **BETCHA!**

Panel 6:

NO, NO, NO, NO, NO!!

OK, I'LL DO IT.

BUT **DAD,** IF **YOU** DON'T AGREE TO BE THE BACK-UP LAMAZE COACH, THEN, I GUESS WE'LL HAVE TO ASK **DEBBIE'S DAD.**

...THIS IS THE RIGHT ROOM NUMBER, BUT NO LAMAZE CLASS. MAYBE WE'RE JUST A LITTLE EARLY.

OR JUST MAYBE THIS IS THE WRONG BUILDING.

ROOM 4A

NO. THIS IS MOST DEFINITELY THE RIGHT ROOM AND THE RIGHT BUILDING...

AGGGH!!

OH, I'M SORRY, I DIDN'T MEAN TO GIVE YOU A FRIGHT. AFTER ALL, WE DO WANT TO SEE JUNIOR GO TO FULL TERM, DON'T WE.

...I'M NURSE MIKE, BY THE WAY, THE NATURAL CHILDBIRTH SPECIALIST FROM THE HOSPITAL. I'LL BE YOUR LAMAZE INSTRUCTOR.

ROOM 4A

CLICK

MAN, YOU NEARLY SCARED THE LIVIN' CRAP OUT O' US!

NOW, NOW, I'VE OFTEN BEEN TOLD THAT MY LOOKS INSPIRE GREAT PASSIONS. HOWEVER, THE MERE SIGHT OF ME IS HARDLY SUFFICIENT TO RENDER ONE'S BOWELS USELESS.

OH YEAH? NOT FROM WHERE I'M STANDING! I MEAN, WHAT COULD BE SCARIER THAN BEIN' IN A STRANGE, DARK PLACE, TURNIN' AROUND AND SEEIN' SOME BIG, MEAN LOOKIN' BIKER STANDIN' OVER YOU?

TIM BARELA

...WHY ARE YOU HERE AT ALL, TO BEGIN WITH? THE KIDS DIDN'T ASK YOU TO BE THE BACK-UP LAMAZE COACH, THEY ASKED ME!

BECAUSE, IT'S A FATHER'S DUTY TO PROTECT HIS UNBORN GRANDSON FROM HIS DAUGHTER'S FOOLISHNESS!

WILL YOU TWO, PLEASE, JUST SHUT-UP?! WE NEVER SHOULD'VE ASKED OR SAID ANYTHING TO ANYBODY!

OH YEAH? AND JUST WHAT DO YOU MEAN BY THAT?

IF ANYONE'S GOING TO BE MY NEW GRANDSON'S VERY FIRST MALE INFLUENCE, IT'S GOING TO BE A NORMAL PERSON, NOT SOME SEXUAL DEVIANT!

OH YEAH?! I SWEAR, WHEN THE TIME COMES, I'M GONNA LOCK MYSELF IN THE BATHROOM AND HAVE THIS KID IN THE TUB!

ROOM 4A

THE ANSWER TO YOUR QUESTION MAY HAVE JUST WALKED THROUGH THE DOOR.

Panel 1:

...UNLIKE YOUR CHEAP, PLASTIC WATCH, MY ROLEX HAS BUILT-IN MEMORY, ALARM AND STOP WATCH FUNCTIONS. IF ANYONE'S TO MONITOR THE CONTRACTIONS, IT SHOULD BE ME.

OH? AND AT WHICH SWAP MEET DID YOU MANAGE TO FIND THAT TACKY, GOLD PLATED, TAIWANESE RIP-OFF ANYWAY?

Panel 2:

GENTLEMEN, PLEASE! THIS IS, AFTER ALL, A LAMAZE CLASS, NOT AN EPISODE OF "FAMILY FEUD" MEETS "LIFESTYLES OF THE MIDDLE-CLASS AND PRETENTIOUS"!

...AND YOU, MR. EVANS, I WOULD NOT PRESUME TO BE QUITE SO SMUG IF I WERE YOU. I HAVE NOT FORGOTTEN WHAT HAPPENED FOUR YEARS AGO, YOUR FIRST RIDE ON THE GRANDPARENT MERRY-GO-ROUND.

Panel 3:

...I REMEMBER HOW YOUR BACKBONE TURNED TO JELLO AND HOW YOU DESERTED YOUR FAMILY JUST WHEN THEY AND YOUR FIRST GRANDCHILD NEEDED YOU THE MOST...

IF YOUR PRESENCE HERE IS SOME FEEBLE ATTEMPT AT REDEMPTION, YOU'LL HAVE TO MAKE A MORE CONVINCING EFFORT THAN THIS!

THAT'S RIGHT.

Panel 4:

WE WILL CONTEND WITH YOU LATER.

Panel 5:

ALRIGHT, MR. EVANS, YOU ARE IN THE DELIVERY ROOM. YOUR SON IS NOT AVAILABLE, YOUR DAUGHTER-IN-LAW IS IN LABOR AND IN NEED OF YOUR ASSISTANCE. BY YOUR "CHEAP, PLASTIC WATCH" YOU CAN TELL THAT THE CONTRACTIONS ARE A MERE THREE MINUTES APART. WHAT DO YOU DO?

WELL, I, UH...

Panel 6:

BREATHING EXERCISES, MR. EVANS, BREATHING EXERCISES: HEE, HEE—HOO, HOO! THE CONTRACTIONS ARE COMING FASTER AND FASTER! YOUR DAUGHTER-IN-LAW IS NOW COMPLETELY DILATED—THERE'S THE BABY'S HEAD! WHAT DO YOU DO?

HEE, HEE HEE—HOO, HOO... HEE, HEEE...

JIM BARELA

Panel 7:

HEEE! HEE! HEEEE!

OH GAWD, HE'S HYPERVENTILATING!

THEY DON'T PAY ME ENOUGH TO PUT UP WITH THIS BULL SHIT.

Panel 1:
"TELL LEONARD THE **TRUTH**, DADDY— **EVERYTHING** THAT HAPPENED— OR I'LL HAVE **NURSE MIKE** KICK YOUR **BUTT** THROUGH THAT **PLATE GLASS** WINDOW!"

"AND IT WOULD INDEED BE MY PLEASURE."

"WELL, I DON'T REALLY KNOW WHERE TO START."

"WHY NOT TRY AT THE **BEGINING**!"

(Newspaper: Register — TV EVANGELIST DIES OF STROKE ON THE AIR — SALE! SALE! — BOSNIA HEATS UP)

Panel 2:
"WELL, WHEN LARRY GOT HERE, AFTER HE TOOK RICHARD TO THE AIRPORT, WE SORT'VE GOT INTO ONE OF OUR LITTLE **ARGUMENTS**. YOU KNOW, THE USUAL, ABOUT HIM NOT BEING A PROPER **ROLE MODEL** FOR MY NEW **GRANDSON**, ABOUT HIM WEARING THAT "GAY & LESBIAN PARENTS" T-SHIRT IN THE DELIVERY ROOM. I GUESS WE GOT KINDA **LOUD**. I GUESS **THEY** OVERHEARD US AND **FOLLOWED** LARRY OUT TO THE PARKING LOT... HE FORGOT THIS THING. RICHARD BOUGHT IT FOR DEBBIE AT THE AIRPORT."

"DO YOU, AT LEAST, KNOW WHAT "THEY" LOOK LIKE? HOW MANY WERE "THEY"?"

(Balloon: "I Love You!")

Panel 3:
"I DON'T KNOW!...TWO, MAYBE **THREE** OF THEM. THEY WERE **REDNECK** TYPES, I SUPPOSE; NOT A NICE LOOKING BUNCH, THAT'S FOR SURE."

"WELL, I WANT TO SEE HIM. WHERE IS LARRY?"

"MR. **EVANS** IS IN THE ER UNDERGOING EVALUATION. BUT **YOU CAN'T** GO IN THERE."

(Signature: TIM BARELA)

Panel 4:
"BUT I HAVE TO SEE HIM! WHY CAN'T I GO IN THERE?"

"HOSPITAL **RULES**, SIR— **IMMEDIATE FAMILY ONLY**. THE **ONLY** WAY YOU MIGHT BE ALLOWED TO GO BACK THERE AND GET IN THE DOCTOR'S WAY IS IF YOU WERE **MARRIED** TO MR. EVANS."

"BUT WE ARE! NOT LEGALLY, OF COURSE, BUT...SEE THE RING?"

Panel 5:
"RULES ARE RULES, SIR. BESIDES, THIS HOSPITAL DOES NOT RECOGNIZE SUCH AN "ARRANGEMENT" AS BEING A **VALID** DOMESTIC RELATIONSHIP."

"NOT "VALID"? NOT "VALID"?! LOOK LADY, I HAVE LIVED WITH AND FOUGHT WITH AND PUT-UP WITH AND LOVED THAT MAN FOR MORE THAN FIFTEEN YEARS. YOU CANNOT JUST DISMISS US AND OUR RELATIONSHIP WITH THE WAVE OF SOME STUPID, NARROW MINDED, ASININE LITTLE "RULE"!!"

Panel 6:
"GOOD GOD, AT LEAST LET ME KNOW WHAT'S GOING ON BACK THERE!"

Panel 7:
"DOCTOR! I'M LOSING MR. EVAN'S VITAL SIGNS!"

"DON'T BE RIDICULOUS, NURSE, MR. EVANS MERELY HAS A LITTLE CONCUSS..."

"DOCTOR! MR. EVANS IS FLATLINING!!"

"OOPS."

(Sign: ER RESTRICTED ADMITTANCE)

...LOOK, I'VE GOT THIS DEAD GUY—WHO'S NOT SUPPOSED TO BE—STANDING HERE AND YOU'RE TELLING ME THAT IT'S A SOFTWEAR SCREW-UP? AGAIN?!

...WELL WHY DOES THE PURCHASING DEPARTMENT INSIST ON BUYING THAT CRAPPY SOFTWEAR? THOSE PEOPLE AREN'T THE ONLY SOFTWEAR COMPANY IN THE UNIVERSE, THEY JUST SEEM LIKE IT!

...WELL, FOR ALL THE JOY HE'S GIVEN US, WE'LL BE SURE TO RESERVE A WARM SPOT FOR A CERTAIN MR. GATES!

MR. EVANS, WE ARE SO SORRY ABOUT THIS LITTLE INCONVENIENCE. WE'RE WORKING ON THE PROBLEM AND SHOULD HAVE YOU BACK....

WAIT A MINUTE, THIS IS HEAVEN, RIGHT? AND I'M DEAD, RIGHT? SO WHY AM I HERE? I MEAN, I AM GAY, AFTER ALL.

PARDON ME, MR. EVANS, BUT I DON'T QUITE FOLLOW YOUR...

I WAS ALWAYS TOLD THAT GAY PEOPLE DON'T GO TO HEAVEN.

OH, DON'T BE SILLY! OF COURSE GAY PEOPLE GET TO GO TO HEAVEN IF THEY WANT TO.

WHY, JUST LOOK AT THIS GORGEOUS PLACE; WE'VE HAD SOME OF THE BEST INTERIOR DECORATORS IN THE BUSINESS COME THRU HERE!

...NOT TO MENTION ALL THE FABULOUS GOURMET FOOD, OPERA AND BROADWAY REVIVALS!

BUT...

NO BUTS!...LOOK, WE KNOW THAT YOU'RE GAY. WE EVEN KNOW ABOUT YOUR "EXOTIC" TASTES AND FETISHES. SO? YOU DIDN'T INVENT HUMAN SEXUALITY. IS A PERSON RESPONSIBLE FOR THE COLOR OF THEIR EYES OR WHETHER THEY'RE RIGHT OR LEFT HANDED? A PERSON DOESN'T COME HERE OR GO TO THE OTHER PLACE BECAUSE OF WHO THEY SLEPT WITH. WHAT'S IN YOUR HEART, THAT'S WHAT REALLY MATTERS...

BLASPHEMY! I HAVE HEARD JUST ABOUT ENOUGH BLASPHEMY TA LAST AN ETERNITY! THAT LOATHSOME SEXUAL PERVERT IS RIGHT! HE DOES NOT BELONG HERE, BUT I DO!!

WHY ARE YOU EVEN TALKIN' TA THAT DAMNABLE SINNER, WASTIN' PRECIOUS TIME WHEN I, A RIGHTEOUS MAN, HAVE BEEN FORCED TA SIT HERE AND WAIT?! I WANT SOME SERVICE! I WANT TA GO ON TA MY REWARD!!

FUNDIES!—THAT ONE'S A SO-CALLED "TELEVISION EVANGELIST," DID THE ALMIGHTY A BIG FAVOR LAST NIGHT WHEN HE HAD A STROKE DURING ONE OF HIS BROADCASTS—I SWEAR, THEY ARE THE WORST! THEY THINK THEY OWN THIS PLACE!

TIM BARELA

...BUT YOU WERE REAL NICE TA THAT PERSON 'N' HE'S NOT EVEN SUPPOSED TA BE HERE! I JUST WANT WHAT'S COMIN' TA ME, TA GO ON TA MY HEAVENLY REWARD.

OH, BUT YOU ALREADY HAVE YOUR "REWARD". DON'T YOU REMEMBER WHAT WAS WRITTEN ABOUT THE PHARISEES? HOW THEY ALL LOVED TO IMPRESS PEOPLE WITH THEIR "HOLINESS" BY PRAYING AND PONTIFICATING IN PUBLIC?..."THEY HAVE THEIR REWARD."...YOU DID THE SAME SORT'VE THING ON TV—WHAT, YOU WERE EXPECTING, MAYBE, A MEDAL?

BUT I WAS A BAPTIST PREACHER, A CHRISTIAN! I WASN'T ANYTHIN' LIKE THOSE PEOPLE!

YOU WERE EVERYTHING LIKE "THOSE PEOPLE" YOUR ILK ARE THE PHARISEES OF YOUR AGE: DECLARING YOUR'S TO BE THE ONLY TRUE INTERPRETATION OF SCRIPTURE, CONTROLLING THE LIVES OF YOUR TRUSTING FOLLOWERS, EVEN TELLING THEM HOW TO VOTE WHILE LINING YOUR POCKETS WITH THEIR MONEY! SO MANY OF THE PASSAGES REFERING TO THE PHARISEES APPLY, LET'S TRY A FEW AND SEE HOW WELL THE SHOE FITS...

GOING DOWN?

"HYPOCRITES, BLIND GUIDES, A BREED OF VENOMOUS SNAKES, WHITEWASHED CRYPTS FULL OF ALL MANNER OF DEATH AND PUTRIFICATION"!

WAIT A MINUTE! THINGS WEREN'T SUPPOSED TA TURN OUT THIS WAY! I WANNA TALK TA SOMEONE IN CHARGE... LORD? LORD CAN YOU HEAR ME?...PLEASE!!

"NOT EVERYONE WHO CRIES 'LORD, LORD' SHALL ENTER THE KINGDOM OF HEAVEN. HE WILL TELL THEM, 'I NEVER KNEW YOU; DEPART FROM ME, YOU WHO WORK INIQUITY!'"

..."AND THEY WILL BE CAST INTO THE OUTER DARKNESS WHERE THERE WILL BE WAILING AND GNASHING OF TEETH."

STEP TO THE BACK OF THE CAR PLEASE!

BUT, WHEN I HAD MY STROKE, THEY TOOK MY DENTURES OUT 'N' LEFT 'EM AT THE TV STUDIO! I DON'T HAVE ANY TEETH!!!

OH, I WOULDN'T WORRY ABOUT THAT. TEETH WILL BE PROVIDED.

WOW, WAS THAT A GLASS BOTTOM ELEVATOR? WAS THAT REALLY FIRE AND BRIMSTONE DOWN THERE?

OH NO, JUST SPECIAL EFFECTS. HE IS GOING TO THE OTHER PLACE, BUT HE'LL BE SPENDING ETERNITY LOCKED IN A VERY SMALL ROOM WITH LEONA HELMSLEY, NANCY REAGAN, IMELDA MARCOS AND ZSA ZSA GABOR. AFTER TEN MINUTES IN THERE HE'LL BE BEGGING US TO DOUSE HIM WITH GASOLINE AND GIVE HIM A MATCH...BUT WE WON'T DO IT.

Panel 1:
WELL, WE'VE HAD A BUSY DAY, HAVEN'T WE? BUT ALL GOOD THINGS, ALL TOO SOON, MUST COME TO AN END. ALL EXCEPT YOUR LIFE, THAT IS, WHICH WASN'T SUPPOSED TO BE OVER QUITE THIS SOON. IT'S TIME TO SEND YOU BACK.

NOW, I WANT YOU TO CLOSE YOUR EYES, CLICK YOUR HEELS TOGETHER THREE TIMES AND SAY, "THERE'S NO PLACE LIKE BOY'S TOWN, THERE'S NO PLACE LIKE BOY'S TOWN..."

HUH?

Panel 2:
AW C'MON! I'VE ALWAYS WANTED TO DO THAT WITH SOMEONE LIKE YOU.

BUT WHAT IF I DON'T WANT TO GO BACK? WHAT IF I WANT TO STAY AND SEE WHAT'S ON UP AHEAD?

NOW, YOU'RE NOT GOING TO START BEING DIFFICULT, ARE YOU? TRUST ME, YOU'LL HAVE PLENTY OF TIME TO CHECK OUT THE REST OF THIS PLACE ON YOUR NEXT VISIT.

Panel 3:
BUT I FEEL "RIGHT" HERE, COMFORTABLE. SUDDENLY MY LIFE MAKES SENSE AND I UNDERSTAND MY REASON FOR BEING. I BELONG HERE. I DON'T WANT TO GO BACK.

BUT YOU HAVE TO GO BACK. YOU DON'T BELONG HERE QUITE YET. OF COURSE, ALL THAT'S JUST A MATTER OF TIME AND CIRCUMSTANCE,—YOUR TIMELY DEMISE OR THE CARTOONIST'S, WHICHEVER COMES FIRST.

BUT WOULD MY STAYING MAKE THAT MUCH DIFFERENCE? UPSET SOME GREAT COSMIC PLAN? WHY DO I NEED TO GO BACK TO ALL THAT PAIN 'N' SUFFERING, ALL THE HATE 'N' PREJUDICE IN THE WORLD THAT PUT ME HERE IN THE FIRST PLACE? WHY? GIVE ME ONE GOOD REASON.

I CAN GIVE YOU SEVERAL, AT LEAST A FEW OTHER PEOPLE WHO STILL WANT AND NEED YOU IN THEIR LIVES: YOUR FRIENDS AND EMPLOYEES, YOUR FAMILY, YOUR CHILDREN AND GRANDCHILDREN...OH YES, AND ONE SPECIAL PERSON IN PARTICULAR...TAKE A LOOK.

Panel 4:
...HE'S BEEN WORRIED SICK, YOU KNOW. HE'S BEEN WAITING FOR YOU ALL NIGHT. HE LOVES YOU VERY, VERY MUCH...

LEONARD! I FORGOT ALL ABOUT LEONARD! I'M SORRY, SWEETHEART, I NEED YOU, TOO! I'M COMING BACK FOR YOU. I'M COMING BACK!

...I LOVE YOU!...

Panel 5:
YUP, GET'S 'EM EVERY TIME. ONE MINUTE THEY'RE HERE, THE NEXT...POOF!

WELL, SEND UP THE NEXT ONE, TOD.

RIGHT, BOSS.

80

81

...WELL, SINCE **I** OWN THE PIANO AND LIVE IN **BELMONT HIEGHTS** AND WE'LL, INITIALLY, BE DOING ALL OUR PRACTICE SESSIONS AND REHEARSALS HERE, I SAY THAT WE SHOULD CALL OURSELVES "**THE BELMONT TRIO**"...SHALL WE BEGIN WITH THE DVOŘÁK OR THE **SAINT-SAËNS**?

HOW ABOUT "THE DVOŘÁK TRIO" OR "THE **SAINT-SAËNS** TRIO" OR SOMETHING LIKE THAT?

NO WAY. MOST PEOPLE CAN'T EVEN **PRONOUNCE** DVOŘÁK OR SAINT-SAËNS! BESIDES, THERE'S ALREADY "**TOO MANY**" "BORODIN" TRIOS AND "**ALBAN BERG**" QUARTETS LURKING AROUND OUT THERE. I DON'T WANT TO BE STUCK WEARING THE NAME OF SOME DEAD COMPOSER LIKE A **BAD TOUPEE.** I'D PREFER SOMETHING **AMBIGUOUS**, EVEN SOMETHING **MYSTERIOUS** AND **CRYPTIC**. "BELMONT TRIO" ISN'T BAD. ...HOW ABOUT THE DVOŘÁK?

BEEP BEEP BEEP! BEEP BEEP BEEP!

OOPS, THAT'S MINE.

HELLO?...OH, HELLO SON. I HOPE THAT THIS IS **IMPORTANT. DADDY** IS IN REHEARSAL. YOU KNOW THAT I'VE TOLD YOU, **TIME** AND TIME AGAIN, **NOT** TO CALL DADDY WHEN HE'S IN REHEARSAL.

...OH...**REALLY?** ...WELL THAT'S **WONDERFUL!** YES, DADDY IS **VERY PROUD** OF HIS **LITTLE BOY!**

...ALRIGHT SON, DADDY HAS TO GET BACK TO HIS REHEARSAL NOW. THE OTHER NICE GENTLEMEN ARE WAITING...**WHAT?**

...**NO.** YOU KNOW **THE RULES.** YOU CANNOT HAVE YOUR **PLAYMATES** OVER TO VISIT WHEN **DADDY'S AWAY...NO,** DADDY WANTS TO BE THERE TO **SUPERVISE** YOUR **PLAYTIME...YES,** WE'LL DISCUSS THIS FURTHER WHEN DADDY GETS HOME. ...YES, WE'LL SEE YOU THEN. GOOD-BYE.

I DIDN'T KNOW THAT YOU HAVE **KIDS.**

I DON'T.

I **KNOW!** HOW ABOUT "**MÉNAGE À TROIS**"?

GET REAL!

AW GEEZ!!

WELL, I LIKE IT.

JASON LEE! PLEASE PUT MR. PACK MAN TOAD BACK IN HIS AQUARIUM THIS INSTANT! WE DON'T WANT HIM GETTING LOOSE AND TRYING TO EAT MR. HAMSTER AGAIN, NOW DO WE?

...I WANT YOU BACK AT YOUR PLACE AND WORKING TO FINISH YOUR "FAMILY TREE" PROJECT LIKE ALL THE OTHER CHILDREN. ...RIGHT NOW!

CLASS, GET YOUR DRAWINGS READY. I'M GOING TO BE COMING AROUND WITH MY BIG RED MARKER AND WRITING NAMES UNDER ALL THE LOVELY PICTURES OF YOUR NICE RELATIVES.

MY MY, LAUREN, ISN'T YOUR DRAWING JUST WONDERFUL! NOW, TELL ME EXACTLY WHO ALL THESE SPECIAL PEOPLE ARE.

WELL, THIS IS MY MOMMY 'N' DADDY 'N' THIS IS MICHAEL, MY BRAN' NEW BABY BROTHER. THIS IS MY GRAMMA BARBRA 'N' MY GRAMPA PHIL. THEY'RE MY MOMMY'S MOMMY 'N' DADDY.

...THIS ONE'S MY GRAMMA SHARON 'N' THIS IS MY GRAMPA LARRY 'N' MY GRAMPA LEONARD.

OH MY, THREE GRANDFATHERS? YOU KNOW, LAUREN, MOST CHILDREN ONLY HAVE TWO.

WELL, YA SEE, THIS ONE 'N' THIS ONE USED TA BE MARRIED. USED TA BE, BUT NOT ANY MORE. THEY'RE MY DADDY'S MOMMY 'N' DADDY.

OH, I SEE. YOUR GRANDMOTHER SHARON IS REMARRIED NOW TO YOUR GRANDFATHER LEONARD.

NO. MY GRAMPA LARRY 'N' MY GRAMPA LEONARD ARE THE ONES THAT GOT MARRIED.

NOW LAUREN, DON'T BE SILLY! GRANDFATHERS DO NOT AND CANNOT MARRY EACH OTHER!

SURE THEY CAN, MISS ARBORGAS! I WAS THERE. I WAS THE FLOWER GIRL 'N' EVERYTHING!

OH, I SEE... AND THESE TWO, ARE THEY MARRIED AS WELL?

AW, DON'T BE SILLY MISS ARBORGAS!

...MY GRAMPA LARRY SAYS THAT MY UNCLE DAVID AND MY UNCLE COLLIN ARE "JUST SHAKIN' UP TILL THEY SET THE DATE."

OF COURSE, HOW SILLY OF ME.

THAT'S COLLIN WITH TWO "L's".

WOW. OUR FIRST PARENT/TEACHER CONFERENCE AND **WE'RE** THE PARENTS. I GUESS IT'S **OFFICIAL**, WE'RE **REALLY** GROWN-UPS NOW.

...I KNOW THAT **LAUREN** CAN BE A HANDFUL. SHE'S REALLY BRIGHT AND, FOR A KINDERGARTENER, SHE ALREADY KNOWS HER NUMBERS AND LETTERS AND CAN READ A LITTLE. SHE **REPEATS** EVERYTHING LIKE A **PARROT**...IS THAT IT? WAS IT SOMETHING THAT LAUREN **SAID?**

WELL, LAST WEEK THE CHILDREN WERE DRAWING PICTURES OF THEIR RELATIVES, MAKING A LITTLE "FAMILY TREE". THAT'S WHEN LAUREN TOLD ME ABOUT HER **TWO MARRIED GRANDFATHERS**, BEING THE FLOWER GIRL IN THEIR "**WEDDING**." AND LET'S NOT FORGET THE TWO **UNCLES** WHO ARE "**JUST SHACKIN' UP**."

OH BOY.

YUP, MY DAD AND MY BROTHER, THEY'RE **BOTH GAY**...I GUESS THAT SORT'VE MAKES **ME** THE "**BLACK SHEEP**" OF THE FAMILY.

NOW, I'VE BEEN TRYING VERY HARD TO **UNDERSTAND** ALL THIS. HOW LOVING PARENTS COULD **ALLOW** THEIR CHILDREN TO BE **EXPOSED** TO SUCH PEOPLE, ALL THE POTENTIAL **DETRIMENTAL** EFFECTS. MY CHURCH PASTOR RECOMMENDED SOME **BOOKS** ABOUT **HOMOSEXUAL PRACTICES**...

WHAT?! LOOK LADY, THE ONLY THING WE'VE "**ALLOWED**" LAUREN TO BE "**EXPOSED TO**" IS HER OWN **FAMILY!** LAUREN'S UNCLE AND GRANDFATHER **LOVE** HER. THERE'S **NOTHING DIRTY** OR "**DETRIMENTAL**" ABOUT **THAT!** RIGHT RICHARD?

WELL, YEAH.

...LARRY AND DAVID WOULD **NEVER DREAM** OF SAYING OR DOING OR "**PRACTICING**" **ANYTHING** IN FRONT OF LAUREN THAT WOULD EFFECT OR HURT HER IN **ANY WAY!** TELL HER ABOUT **YOUR** FATHER AND BROTHER!

WELL, UH...

THEN WHAT ABOUT **LAUREN'S** DRAWING? WHAT ABOUT THIS PICTURE OF HER TWO GRANDFATHERS AND THIS **HAIRY LITTLE MAN** BEING LEAD AROUND IN **BLACK LEATHER** AND **CHAINS?**

THAT'S **NOT** A "HAIRY LITTLE MAN", THAT'S LAUREN'S **TEDDY BEAR**..IT WAS DAD'S GIFT TO HER WHEN SHE WAS BORN.

TEDDIES IN BONDAGE FOR **NEWBORNS?!** ARE YOU PEOPLE **SICK?!!**

OK, SO WHAT SHOULD I TELL HER **NOW?**

LEONARD, DO WE STILL HAVE ONE OF THOSE OLD CIGARS THAT RICHARD WAS PASSING OUT WAY BACK WHEN LAUREN WAS BORN?

GEEZ, I DON'T KNOW! IF WE DO, IT'S PROBABLY SHOVED TO THE BACK OF SOME DRAWER, SOMEWHERE. WHY?

WELL, I WAS THINKING THAT, IF I COULD STICK A CIGAR IN THE BABY'S MOUTH RIGHT NOW, HE'D LOOK JUST LIKE WINSTON CHURCHILL.

REC

IF YOU WOULDN'T LET MICHAEL PICK AT THE GRASS AND PUT BUGS IN HIS MOUTH HE WOULDN'T HAVE THAT EXPRESSION.

GRAMPA, ARE YOU MAKIN' FUN OF MY BABY BROTHER?

OH, OF COURSE NOT, PUNKIN! ...COM'ERE 'N' SIT DOWN, SWEETHEART, GRAMPA WANTS TO TALK TO YOU.

AM I IN TROUBLE?

NO, YOU'RE NOT IN TROUBLE. ...YOUR PARENTS SHOWED ME THE "FAMILY TREE" THAT YOU MADE IN SCHOOL, ALL THOSE WONDERFUL DRAWINGS OF YOU 'N' YOUR MOM 'N' DAD, YOUR BROTHER, YOUR GRAMMAS 'N' GRAMPAS 'N' AUNTS 'N' UNCLES.

...THEY ALSO TOLD ME THAT, WHEN YOU DREW IT, YOU TOLD YOUR TEACHER ALL ABOUT YOUR GRAMPA LEONARD 'N' ME, HOW WE LIVE TOGETHER 'N' HOW WE GOT MARRIED HERE IN THE BACK YARD A COUPLE OF YEARS AGO.

...SHE GOT VERY UPSET AND MADE A GREAT BIG FUSS OVER ALL THAT, YOU KNOW.

BUT WHY, GRAMPA?

WELL SWEETHEART, SOME PEOPLE ARE FUNNY THAT WAY. THEY HAVE A HARD TIME ACCEPTING THE FACT THAT OTHER PEOPLE MIGHT BE A LITTLE DIFFERENT THAN THEY ARE. THEY CAN'T OR DON'T WANT TO UNDERSTAND AND THEY BECOME VERY ANGRY.

JIM BROELA

...IN FACT, SOME PEOPLE BECOME SO ANGRY AND SO HATEFUL, THEY DO TERRIBLE THINGS... REMEMBER HOW THOSE NASTY MEN HURT GRAMPA SO BADLY THAT HE HAD TO STAY IN THE HOSPITAL WHEN MICHAEL WAS BORN? THAT'S HOW ANGRY AND HATEFUL SOME PEOPLE CAN BE.

...NOW, IT'S NOT THAT GRAMPA WANTS YOU TO START LYING TO PEOPLE. HE DOES, HOWEVER, WANT YOU TO UNDERSTAND THAT IT CAN BE A BIG, BAD WORLD OUT THERE AND SOMETIMES, UNFORTUNATELY, YOU HAVE TO BE CAREFUL WHO YOU TELL THE TRUTH TO.

WELL, THEN WHAT ABOUT THE OTHER DAY WHEN MY FRIEND DORITA 'N' ME SAW OUR TEACHER, MISS ARBORGAS, AND THE CUSTODIAN, MR. SANCHEZ, KISSIN' IN THE FUTILITY ROOM?

SWEETHEART, YOU HAVE MY PERMISSION TO TELL ABSOLUTELY EVERYBODY ABOUT THAT.

LARRY, EAT A BUG!

...WELL, WE'LL JUST FINISH SETTING UP AND THEN WE'LL START WITH A FEW QUICK POLAROIDS TO MAKE SURE WE HAVE THE LIGHTING AND COMPOSITION THE WAY WE WANT IT.

SOUNDS GOOD TO ME.

I HATE POSING FOR PUBLICITY PHOTOS.

NO PUBLICITY PHOTOS EQUALS ONE UNHAPPY BOOKING AGENT AND NO GIGS FOR THE NEW BELMONT TRIO. ...WHERE'S SKIP?

AROUND HERE SOMEPLACE; HE HAD TO MAKE A PHONE CALL.

...WHAT DO YOU MEAN, "IT JUST SLIPPED MY MIND"? HE'S BEEN IN THERE FOR HOURS AND YOU HAVEN'T EVEN BOTHERED TO CHECK AND SEE IF HE'S OK?

...WELL YES, CERTAINLY, AT LEAST OPEN THE DOOR AND SEE IF HE NEEDS WATER OR SOMETHING...GOOD. NOW REMEMBER SON, WHILE DADDY'S AWAY HIS CARE IS ENTIRELY IN YOUR HANDS. OH YES, AS FAR AS HIS TRUSSING IS CONCERNED...

...WHEN IT'S TIME TO LET HIM OUT, BE SURE TO UNTIE HIM VERY CAREFULLY. HIS SKIN IS SURE TO BE QUITE TENDER AFTER HIS ORDEAL AND I DON'T WANT TOO MANY MARKS SHOWING WHEN HE'S ON DISPLAY FOR OUR GUESTS THIS EVENING.

WHA- WHA- WHAT IS WITH YOU PEOPLE?!!

...YOU KNOW, I CONSIDER MYSELF A RATHER PROGRESSIVE, OPEN MINDED SORT OF PERSON. I WORK AND AM FRIENDS WITH LOTS OF GAY PEOPLE. I IGNORE BOB'S LOVER'S KINKY FETISHES, I PUT UP WITH THEIR FRIEND WITH THE LEATHER SHOP AND THE ROVING EYES. BUT THIS...THE PROPER CARE AND FEEDING OF SOME S&M TRICK, TIED UP IN SOME CLOSET SOMEWHERE, ONLY TO BE LET OUT AND PUT "ON DISPLAY" FOR THE PLEASURE OF YOUR "GUESTS"?!! GOOD GAWWD MAN, HOW...HOW...

"TRICK"? WE'RE TALKING ABOUT A DUCK.

...WE'VE BEEN SLOW ROASTING A DUCK IN THE OVEN SINCE THIS MORNING. WE'RE HAVING DINNER GUESTS OVER TONIGHT.

GOOD GRIEF GENE, JUST LOOK AT YOU! THEY'RE GOING TO HAVE TO DO YOUR HAIR AND MAKE-UP ALL OVER AGAIN!

SON, MAKE A NOTE FOR ME: IF WE EVER HAVE EUGENE OVER FOR SUPPER, VEGITARIAN CUISINE ONLY.

TIM BARELA

Leonard & Larry Volume I

Domesticity Isn't Pretty

$ 12.95 (ISBN 1-884568-00-9)